THE TWISTED TOMAHAWK

by Steve A. Zuckerman

This book is dedicated to the brave men and women of the United
States Coast Guard who tirelessly work to protect lives and property
wherever their missions take them.
Semper Paratus-Always Ready

Other Books by Steve A. Zuckerman

Djinn and Tonnick Murder Mysteries
        The Ruthless Relic
        The Twisted Tomahawk
        The Vindictive Vines

The Alien Roadkill Series
        Dealbreaker-Book 1
        Homecoming-Book 2
        Realization-Book 3
        Blowback-Book 4
        Betrayal-Book 5
        Confrontation-Book 6

CHAPTER ONE

An Iviatim Battle Circle, North America. 500 B.C.

ALBOK HURLED HIS WEAPON at the same moment he dodged the spear that aimed squarely at his chest. Twisting his body sideways at the last moment, the sharp fire-hardened tip of the wooden missile left a bloody furrow where it grazed past Albok's ribcage. Tacquish, The warrior who had loosed the spear, was not so lucky. The obsidian blade of Albok's ironwood war ax buried itself deeply into Tacquish's forehead with a loud, sickening crack.

The rapidly growing river of dark blood obscured Tacquish's vision, but not the rage that contorted his features as he staggered blindly forward with outstretched hands. It was as if he was hoping to seize Albok and continue the battle he had just lost.

"Balisha notsomu tamaka nupah..." Tacquish hissed, just loud enough for Albok alone to hear. His voice was sibilant, intense and full of menace. The words he muttered were not meant for the ears of the other warriors who had wisely kept themselves at a safe distance from the combat.

Albok drew his bone knife, determined to prevent the Shaman from completing the curse. His blade tore through the other man's throat only too late. The final words had been said; the damage done. His opponent knew this also, and even as he spewed his last breath through the gaping rift in his neck, Tacquish managed a wicked grimace as he collapsed onto the ground.

Ignoring the rapidly expanding puddle of blood that grew near his feet, Albok stood over the body. Though he was utterly spent from his exertions, an involuntary shudder overtook his loud, ragged breathing and pounding heart. He was a hardened warrior, and throughout his unnaturally long life, many men had fallen at his feet. However, the power of the man he had just slain was undeniable. When he looked up at the faces of those who had witnessed the battle, it was apparent to him that even in death, the dark countenance of Tacquish provoked the same fear and dread as it did in life.

There was a moment of unexpected silence as if the onlookers were holding their breath, unsure that the fallen shaman was truly dead. No man was as feared or hated as Tacquish was. Albok looked up at the men who surrounded him. These were some of the fiercest warriors from among the seven bands of the Lakes. They bore the wounds and scars from many battles, and yet they still hung back. As their misgivings slowly passed, the ring of warriors tightened around the challenge circle. They found their courage to draw closer as it became evident to them that the man who had once boasted he would never die—was now truly dead. Then, there was a spontaneous eruption of loud jubilation that rippled through the small Iviatim village. To Albok's ears, the cries expressed more relief than celebration.

Albok took no heed of the accolades that they shouted in his name. His ears were still ringing with the last imprecations which had so softly escaped the shaman's lips. Abruptly, somewhere off in the palms, an owl cried out followed by the peal of distant thunder. The sounds raggedly snuffed out the rejoicing voices of the village as water poured on a cook-fire. From child to elder, every person in the village, had been taught to recognize the significance of the owl's distinctive call. The god, *Muut*, had come to take Tacquish's spirit to Temayuwat in his realm below the earth. *Perhaps*, Albok thought, *this time he'll stay there.*

CHAPTER TWO

Los Angeles, California. Present Day.

I'LL GIVE HER ONE thing—she sure knew how to make an entrance. She strutted into my office with a confident swagger you don't see too often this side of Sunset Boulevard. When she turned those big brown eyes my way, it was as if she was saying, "I own you, mister."

I suppose it was my fault for leaving my office door open, but she was the last thing I would ever expect to come through it. Goddamn stray cat. Surprising, to say the least. Not only because of all the heavy street traffic around the run-down building I'm in—but my office is on the second floor.

So, I figured she'd vanish as fast as she appeared. There wasn't anything here she'd be interested in unless it was a bowl of tequila, and I wasn't in the mood to share. In fact, I wasn't in much of a mood for anything.

It had only been a couple of weeks since I worked one of the strangest cases I had ever undertaken as a PI, and trust me when I tell you that. I'm still not sure I ended up believing half of the crazy that went down. Hell, I'm still processing—and that is an understatement. After that, one thing led to another, and for the first time since I started this lousy career, I am working on a retainer. Not a big one, but it pays the bills. Okay... It's actually a little better than that, seeing I can afford a better grade of tequila and a few free perks too—like no cell phone or Internet bill. All compliments of my benefactor, Bruce Ashton, the CEO of AC&C, which as everyone knows, is the largest telecommunication conglomerate in the world. It might not seem much to anybody with a steady job, but for me, it was like winning the lottery.

As soon as I finished drinking my breakfast, I began contemplating the day's business. I was reasonably sure that by the time I looked up again my furry visitor would resume her travels back out to the street. So with that comforting thought in mind, I set about the tasks at hand.

Today, there wasn't a lot for me to do, but I felt like I should at least try to actually earn the money my client keeps sending me. After all, working on retainer was a whole new experience and a major lifestyle change. The only other time I was enjoyed continuous employment was during my stint in the military—and you can probably guess how that turned out.

Sure, for me Iraq was a real blast, literally. My purple heart is shoved where I don't have to look at it, way at the back of the same desk drawer where I keep my BevMo coupons. I don't like to be reminded of how much luckier I was than the rest of the guys in the Hummer when we ran over the IED. Call it luck, call it a twist of fate —it really makes no difference because in the end, I was the only one who lived through the explosion. By some miracle, I managed to crawl away with all of my limbs intact, and just a single scar, that is, if you don't count all the ones on my psyche.

The scar is on my face where I get to look at it on the days I bother to shave. It's roughly in the shape of a star left by bits of shrapnel which my kooky clients claim are shards of a magic bottle that once contained a genie. You know, the three wishes kind. Supposedly, pieces of that clay pot are permanently embedded in my cheekbone. And, if you think that's hard to swallow, here's one better. One of my client's associates, and most notably, my erstwhile partner—claims to be the container's previous tenant.

Her name is Delinda Djinn, and she's my main contact person with Ashton's company and most likely the one responsible for my generous retainer. I might add that I'm hopelessly obsessed with her, not that she cares. And, personally, I think the whole genie story is bullshit, but as they say, don't bite the hand that pours the tequila, especially when it's as good looking as she is. I don't have to tell you what my three wishes would be—though you probably have a good idea already.

I kept an eye on the cat as it meandered around my messy digs looking for who knows what while I shuffled through the stack of papers on my desk. The pile of paperwork contained the usual stuff that AC&C throws my way. Background checks on new hires, verification of a few disability claims and so on. Nothing very exciting, which is how I like it, or at least that's what I keep telling myself.

I was just going to pour myself another short one when I looked up, and there she was. *Just like magic.* I tried not to act surprised, but the "got-ya" smile on Delinda Djinn's face told me I wasn't pulling it off very well. I would have gestured for her to take a seat, but that would have meant putting down the tequila bottle or the glass, and I wasn't inclined to do either.

"Tonnick, isn't it a little early in the day for that?" Her well-shaped eyebrows were raised in her usual gesture of disdain I'm sure she reserves just for me.

"I got up early. This is lunch," I lied, and she knew it. "Besides, don't you know it's not nice to sneak up on people."

"Your door was open. All I did was come in."

You can't win with her. She's got an explanation for everything.

"You and the cat," I muttered. There was no sign of my feline freeloader. I tried to appear nonchalant. "What's up?"

"We have a meeting with Ashton. Didn't you get my call?" She looked at the blinking light on my answering machine at the same time I did.

"I was just going to check it."

"I called you yesterday." There was that raised eyebrow again. "Ashton is expecting us in twenty minutes. Think you can sober up by then?" She gave me that faint, taunting smile—the same one that haunts me on most nights.

"Before I get sober, I'll need to work more on getting drunk first," I said as I grabbed my jacket off the floor. Hey—I may not be neat, but the upside is everything's easier to find. "Any idea about what Ashton's got on his mind?" Maybe I was about to be fired. If that was the case, Ashton was the kind of guy who'd at least look you in the face when he did it.

"Who's your new friend?" Delinda asked, ignoring me and gesturing at the cat who had just reappeared. She was making herself comfortable on a stack of old newspapers.

"She just wandered in here." I made a move to shoo the damn thing out the door. However, the cat had a different idea and didn't budge.

"How do you know it's a 'she'?" Delinda said coyly.

I made a grab for it, and she darted under the couch with a speed I didn't think possible. "'Cause women seem to have it out for me."

"Come on Mark," Delinda said with just a flicker of amusement. "We've got to go."

I was down on my knees peering under the couch, trying to see where the cat went. "What about the cat?"

"Keep the door open."

"While I'm gone? In this neighborhood? You've got to be kidding!"

Delinda looked around for the half-second she took to appraise the sum total of my worldly possessions. "What do you have that's worth stealing?"

She was right—as usual.

"Only this," I said as I locked the tequila bottle in the desk drawer.

I left the office door ajar just a bit and stopped downstairs at Willy's place. He owns the pawnshop on the bottom floor, and he's my go-to for technical support and the occasional loan. I filled him in about the cat and asked him to keep an eye out for any potential burglars that might be on the prowl for secondhand furniture.

Delinda Djinn and I exited the building's foyer, pushing open the grimy glass doors and stepping out onto the sidewalk. The doors were old and in need of maintenance, like the rest of the place, and shuttered loudly as they swung closed behind us. The building had been an apartment once, built sometime in the late twenties I think. Then, during the fifties when Sunset Boulevard was becoming the de facto entertainment zone around Hollywood, the owner converted it to an office building.

The three upstairs units became offices, and the downstairs units were gutted and made into a couple of storefronts. The secondhand store next to Willy's pawnshop was where I had purchased my office furnishings. It had gone out of business a year or two ago and was still unrented, like the other two offices spaces upstairs. Our part of the Sunset Strip had been left behind as the more prestigious business had moved westward, towards Beverly Hills. This had definitely become the low-rent district—judging from the litter in the gutter and on the sidewalks. I can't remember ever seeing a street-sweeper down here, even though according to the signs, today was a no parking day from 10 AM to noon for street cleaning.

Predictably, Delinda had parked her car right in the middle of the restricted parking zone in front of the building. The car parked behind hers was sporting a traffic ticket tucked neatly tucked under the street-side wiper blade. About thirty feet in front of her Mercedes, a meter maid was industriously completing another ticket for the car parked there. Naturally, Delinda's car was untouched.

"How did she miss you?" I asked, getting into the passenger seat.

"Maybe I'm just lucky..." she replied. "Or, are suggesting I did something magical?"

"You really know how to push my buttons," I remarked as she started the car and jetted out into the stream of traffic, which like most of Los Angeles is nearly impenetrable at just about any time of day.

"Not hard," she demurred. There was that smirk again.

It looked like it was going to be one of those days. First the cat, and now I was a passenger in a car driven by Delinda Djinn—an experience reserved only for those who aren't faint of heart or taking anxiety medication. I only survived the trip to Ashton's Bel-Air estate by keeping my eyes closed much of the way.

Bruce Ashton, the chairman of AC&C, the largest telecom conglomerate in the world, made his home on a sprawling estate. His mansion was discreetly tucked away behind tall, electric wrought-iron gates at the far end of the most expensive neighborhood in the city. As always, the gates opened before we even reached them. Delinda accelerated past them, making short work of the quarter-mile drive through the immaculate and impressively landscaped grounds.

She didn't bother slowing down until we reached the circular driveway in front of the main house. Consequently, I only released my death-grip on the passenger side door handle once the car had shuddered to a complete stop. Delinda had parked the Benz right in front of the massive entry where a familiar figure was making his way down the stairs from the landing to greet us.

"Al, how the hell are you?" I yelled out the window as he came over to the car.

"Good as you'd expect at my age!" Al replied in a voice that sounded like metal scraping on gravel. He opened Delinda's door while giving me the widest grin that his sun-dried and wrinkled face could manage. He was spry despite his years, all things considered. From his looks, you'd probably make him to be about seventy, but you'd be wrong—at least according to him. Al claims to be much, much older. About three thousand years to hear him tell it. I'm sure I've mentioned that my client and his peer group aren't exactly what you'd call ordinary. And having said that, in my opinion, Al is the most normal one of the bunch.

My employer, Bruce Ashton once told me in a serious conversation, that Al is older than that, by about another thousand years or so. Far fetched? You bet, but that's only a taste of what I deal with from time to time. From cursed objects to golems, I've had to navigate situations that don't always lend themselves to rational explanations or happy endings. But frankly, as wacky as these folks are, I have to admit that I like 'em. And, besides, their checks always clear; so how picky can a guy be?

Recently, Al had become Ashton's new head of household owing to the fact the last guy in that position had basically tried to kill us all and nearly succeeded.

"So, how do you like the new job?" I asked.

"Oh, it's fine," he replied, waving the prosthetic right hand that was a souvenir courtesy of his sociopathic predecessor. "Bruce and I get along, and this here's a nice change from my old haunts. Doesn't get nearly as hot."

I gave him a knowing look. He wasn't doing justice to the comparison, considering his former residence was a manufactured home in Death Valley.

Delinda returned his smile as we accompanied him up the steps to the massive stained-oak entry doors. "Is Ashton ready for us?"

"Ready and impatiently waiting... You know better than me how he gets," Al replied as he ushered us into the vestibule and down the hall to the library.

As it always was, the enormous wood-paneled room was dimly lit, owing to Bruce Ashton's aversion to bright light. Even before my eyes made the adjustment, I could tell he was already seated at his desk, the handles of his wheelchair peeking over his slightly slumped shoulders. I knew from experience he could walk if he had to, but chose to conserve his energy for other pursuits.

"Mr. Tonnick, thank you for coming," he said in a voice that was deep and sonorous. It was a perfunctory greeting since we both knew who was paying the freight here. He didn't pause for me to respond.

"A while ago, you might remember I asked if you could set aside your beliefs, or more accurately, your lack of belief, to work on our behalf resolving a serious matter."

"How can I forget," I replied wondering when he'd get to point— you know—the part where he says, "your services are no longer required."

"And despite your personal misgivings, you did so... Admirably, I might add."

Nice touch, I thought, to soften my dismissal with a bit of flattery.

"Thanks," I replied, "but if it wasn't for Delinda..." He didn't let me finish the sentence.

"Indeed, I expected the best from her, but I didn't know what to expect from you."

I couldn't make out Delinda's face in the darkened room, but I'd bet double or nothing for ten bucks she had that smirk going.

"As it turns out, I have another request of you, pretty much along the same lines as before," Ashton continued. "Can we count on your usual cooperation and discretion?"

Truthfully, this turn of events caught me entirely by surprise, although I have to admit, pleasantly—since I wasn't out of a job. At least, not yet.

"Ah, sure," I managed to reply. Apparently, whatever was on Ashton's mind was more pressing than the background checks and the other mundane chores I was currently avoiding. But, even more than that, I was actually curious to see just how far he and Djinn would stretch my credibility this time.

"You sound more surprised than positive, Mr. Tonnick. Did you come here expecting something else?" Ashton almost sounded amused. He added, "Don't worry, we're not done with you yet."

I had a feeling that before this conversation was over, I'd wish I had been right. Unemployment might be better for my health, both mental and otherwise.

"I'm happy to be of service however I can," I said, trying to sound sincere.

"I'm sure you will be, Mr. Tonnick," Ashton said without a trace of humor. "Please keep in mind what I've told you in the past regarding you and Ms. Djinn," he continued. "Whether you truly believe it or not is irrelevant. And, no matter how you feel about that, I'll need the two of you to work together again on this assignment."

I wasn't sure who groaned first, me, or her. The way Ashton tells it, she needs to keep me—or at least the clay shards in my cheek—close by to be the best genie she can be.

Ashton chose to ignore our reactions. He only said, "It will be imperative for both your safety." He reached for the phone on his desk. "Al, please show Mr. Knowle in."

"Mr. Knowle," he explained, "is the reason I asked you here. He'll provide you with some facts on the matter at hand. A matter that could have some financial ramifications for AC&C."

A moment later, Al opened the library door and accompanied the man I presumed was Mr. Knowle into the room. I caught a brief look at the newcomer in the few seconds he remained illuminated in the lighted hallway before Al closed the door.

He was slight of frame, about twenty years older than I—that is to say, he looked to be his early to mid-sixties. He had relatively ordinary features except for his shiny, jet-black hair, which was pulled into a long ponytail that extended far beyond the collar of his gray, pinstriped sports jacket. His body language implied a certain reticence that I assumed was due to him finding himself in such opulent and unfamiliar surroundings. Or, maybe this meeting was cutting into his quality drinking time too.

"Mr. Knowle," Ashton said, "these are my associates, Ms. Delinda Djinn and Mr. Mark Tonnick. They will assist you in resolving this issue. Please have a seat."

In the near darkness, Knowle found one of the empty leather chairs in front of Ashton's desk.

"I apologize for the lack of light, Mr. Knowle, but it affects my eyes adversely."

"No worries, sir. I thank you for taking the time to see me," he responded in a reedy, confident voice with hints of a Hispanic accent. He turned his head towards the chairs where Djinn and I were seated. "Please understand, I'm here at the insistence of our tribal council. While I disagree with their decision to involve AC&C, I'm duty bound as Vice Chairman of the Wiewa Band of Cahuilla Indians to carry out their instructions. They are hopeful you can resolve the matter I'm about to reveal with the utmost discretion."

"You have our assurances," Delinda confirmed in a tone that left no room for doubt. Even though my eyes had not yet adjusted entirely, I got the impression she was looking straight at me when she said it.

There was a pause as Knowle gathered his thoughts. "While it's my personal belief that any action on your part will only complicate the issue, the Tribal Council feels it is best that your company address this directly."

"We have a large stake in your community," Ashton interjected. "The AC&C foundation is the single largest underwriter of the council's ongoing archaeological research. And we've also committed to a sizable donation towards the construction of your new museum in downtown Palm Springs."

"Yes," Knowle responded. "For those reasons, the Tribal Council thinks it best you act to preclude any possible legal remedies against your company," he paused again. If it was for dramatic effect, it was lost on Ashton.

"Please go on, Mr. Knowle," Ashton replied. "You said as much over the phone. Can you provide us with the details?"

"Before I do, I'd like to state my own opinion that much of I'm about to tell you is overblown. After you hear what I have to say, you might decide it is better to let sleeping dogs lie."

"Perhaps," Ashton said. "Once we have all the facts we can evaluate that option."

"Naturally. I'm sure you know that Dr. Howard Schwartz and his team of archeologists have been searching for evidence of early Iviatim settlements throughout the San Jacinto Mountains."

"Certainly," Ashton replied. "It's one of the grants we've funded."

Knowle nodded and hesitated again as if trying to find a way to soft-pedal what was coming next.

"And..." Ashton prompted.

"Dr. Schwartz and his group were searching for petroglyphs and other relics when they stumbled onto evidence of a recent excavation. It was during that discovery they uncovered a buried cable running through Tahquitz Canyon." He paused again as if he had just revealed an earth-shattering secret.

Ashton broke the brief silence by clearing his throat before he spoke. "I have no reason to doubt you Mr. Knowle, but I can assure you our company has no equipment there, unofficially or otherwise. As you're aware, our agreement with your Tribal Council specifically calls for us to bypass the area entirely. No cell towers, no cables or EMF radiators of any kind."

Knowle stood up from his seat and walked over to Ashton's desk. He placed something on it and returned to his chair. "That is one of the cable wraps they found at the site. It has the AC&C logo all over it."

I wasn't sure that Ashton could see clearly enough in the dimly lit room, but evidently he had no difficulty examining it.

"This appears to be one of our branded cable wraps," Ashton hesitantly admitted. "And while I don't understand how it could have gotten there, rest assured we'll look into this matter immediately. If there is even a remote chance that an AC&C conduit has been placed on reservation lands, I'll see that it's removed at once."

"Unfortunately, the damage has already been done," said Knowle. "The council has tried to keep this information from becoming public, but I'm afraid it already has. And now, many tribe members believe your cable is to blame for all the unexplained events and tragedies that have recently afflicted our community."

Knowle waited for a response. When it was clear Ashton wasn't going to comment, Knowle continued. "This has already galvanized nearly every member of the tribe. Many of them are convinced Tahquitz has been awakened... Brought back to life by the energy in the cable. Speaking for myself, I'm not sure there is anything you can do that will undo the damage. In fact, your presence may make matters worse. Only your company's past generosity to the tribe has kept the Tribal Council from tearing up your contract so far... But there is enormous pressure for them to do so."

"I understand," Ashton replied, summoning Al to the room with a button press on his desk phone. "You can be sure we are not taking the situation lightly, and I promise you we will sort all of this out quickly."

"I've been directed to assist in any way I can," said Knowle as he got to his feet.

"That will be greatly appreciated. Ms. Djinn and Mr. Tonnick will arrive to begin their investigation tomorrow. They'll be in contact with you and Dr. Schwarz."

"Of course," Knowle affirmed. He turned to Delinda and I, and added, "I look forward to it."

A moment later, Al cracked the library door open to assist Knowle in exiting the meeting. As soon as the library door closed behind them, Ashton spoke. "So, now you know as much as I do."

"I'm not sure I understand," I asked. "What's the big deal about a phone line? Why would you think that…"

"If you stop talking for a minute, maybe you'll find out," Delinda interjected dryly.

"It's a huge deal, Mr. Tonnick," Ashton said. "The idea that there are any electrical devices in that area is of grave concern to the Native Americans who live in the region. I think you'll find the reasons for that… Interesting."

In the PI business, the word, "interesting" can mean one of several things. None of them good.

Ashton went on. "When you arrive on site tomorrow, ask Knowle to put you in direct contact with Dr. Howard Schwartz. His role is obviously pivotal in this entire affair." He paused to take a breath before he directed his next comment at me. "Mr. Tonnick, let me take a moment to explain the delicate issues that will no doubt complicate your investigation."

I held my tongue, eager for him to get to the point, mainly since he used the words "delicate issues" and "complicate" in the same sentence. There was no question in my mind that things were about to get weird.

"Last year, the US Government demanded that we make available certain equipment and software source code, that according to them, was mandatory under the terms of the Patriot Act. We complied of course as we had no other options."

"Subsequently, several months later we were again contacted and directed to connect an optical trunk line at our substation outside of Palm Springs. Again, we had no other recourse other than to comply. I assumed that could be the cable they've found."

"All right, so the government gets to duke it out with the Indians. Nothing new about that," I observed, thankful for the lack of any supernatural sub-context.

"But there's more. Yesterday, after Knowles called me to request this meeting, I anticipated the subject he wished to discuss, and so I made some inquiries myself. Evidently, Mr. Knowle delayed bringing this to our attention hoping there would be no need for us to be involved. However, after my conversation with the Chairman of the Tribal Council, I contacted the NSA myself and was able to speak with someone at the highest level. They absolutely assured me the optical cable we were directed to splice into our system doesn't run through that area."

"So if they're not lying," I responded, "and the cable doesn't belong to them, and it doesn't belong to you. Whose cable is it?"

"We are talking about the government here, so I, for one, don't discount the possibility they might be lying... But we can't be sure until you check it out." Ashton replied.

"If the government is involved, you can count on some kind of deception," I said flatly, mindful of my own experiences with military intelligence. In my opinion, those two words clearly contradict one another.

"Regardless, you need to find out. What we can't ignore, however, are the strange reports around the San Jacinto area that Knowle was alluding to."

I had to ask even though I knew I'd regret it. "What kind of 'strange' reports are we talking about?"

"I think you know where this is going, don't you Mr. Tonnick?" It was too dark to tell, but I'll bet Ashton had a grin on his face.

Oh shit. Here it comes.

"The reported instances range from sudden disappearances, mysterious noises, cattle deaths and other out of the ordinary events with no apparent explanations."

"Except, I'm sure they are already blaming us," Delinda added.

"I don't get it," I said. "What does a cable have to do with anything? I mean, even if it turns out to be AC&C's cable, this sounds like a meaningless technical violation of a contract." Nobody said anything, so I asked, "And what was Knowle talking about when he spoke of 'waking Tachtree'?"

"Tahquitz," Djinn corrected impatiently. "Don't you get it?"

"Ah... Get what? What am I missing here?"

"I'd say, all of the cultural nuances," Djinn huffed. "As usual."

"That doesn't come up much in my line of work!" I shot back. "Kinda like supernatural events!"

"You wouldn't know one from another, even if they were to fall on top of you and crush you to d..."

"Enough!" Ashton exclaimed. "You're arguing like a married couple."

That did the trick. We both grew instantly silent.

Ashton allowed himself a brief chuckle before he continued. "Let me explain, Mr. Tonnick. The lands the cable supposedly runs through are considered sacred to the Wiewa Band... Extremely sacred." Ashton paused for another deep breath. I figured it was for my benefit. He does that when he's about to make my bullshit meter fly off the scale.

"There is a legend among the Native American people who live in and around the reservation. It speaks of a shaman named Tahquitz... And that his ancient and evil spirit lies asleep somewhere in the San Jacinto Mountains. They believe his timeless and malevolent entity lies waiting for the opportunity to return and wreak havoc on the tribe."

"Seriously? People really believe that?"

Even in the darkness, I saw Ashton nod. "Oh yes. More than you might think. In the 1980s the US Geological Survey unit was scouting the region, intending to run power lines through the area. Once their plans were made public, there was enormous opposition from all of the tribal organizations. They were concerned that energy from the electric wires might awaken the evil spirit, giving it the power to take form. In fact, that objection is documented in the official Environmental Impact Study, which finally concluded it was in everyone's best interest to find other options."

I could picture it now... 'Honey don't run the dishwasher, you'll wake the dead Indian!' Of course, it was utterly preposterous. Still, I could smell a couple days of per-diem coming.

"Okay, are they saying AC&C's cable has caused a bunch of supernatural events?" It was hard not to laugh, but I know from experience that Ashton takes this kind of stuff seriously.

"They are, and if it is our cable, there will be consequences, both financially and socially. That's what you need to find out," he said seriously. "Patriot Act or not, if our cable is really on tribal land, we will only stand to lose utility contracts worth tens of thousands of dollars... But that's not what concerns me. Something is going on down there, and I want you to get to the bottom of it."

I have a hard time imagining what could be more concerning than losing money, but I wasn't about to ask.

"I'm sending Al along with you and Delinda tomorrow. He has, as you will learn, a certain amount of previous history with the matters at hand," Ashton said. Then he added, "Mr. Tonnick, I have prepared a detailed brief for you to review."

Right on cue, Al entered the room and laid a bulging file-folder down on my lap with his trademark toothy grin. When it comes to trolling my skepticism, he loves to twist the knife. "Enjoy..." He quipped before quickly retreating, leaving me to ponder the thick pile of paperwork.

I looked over at Djinn. "Don't you think you should read this first?"

"No. Not really. I think I'll enjoy hearing you tell me all about it on our way down to Palm Springs tomorrow."

Having a conversation about evil spirits with an attractive woman who suffers from a genie delusion would be trying. However, being in a car driven by said lady at the wheel would be even worse. Take my word for it.

CHAPTER THREE

Village of the Two Rivers, North America. 500 B.C.

THERE WAS MUCH DISCUSSION about what should be done with the shaman's corpse. Albok wished to burn it immediately, but the Tribal Elders cautioned that fire might free Tacquish's spirit to exact revenge on the tribe. In the end, they decided that the body would be covered and weighted down with many heavy rocks as to imprison Tacquish until the end of the time of man.

As it was, their fear of the shaman was so great that the warriors of the band drew lots to determine which six of them, besides Albok, would actually touch the body to move it. Albok had no fear of that and even attempted to retrieve the war ax from where it was deeply embedded in Tacquish's skull. However, despite his strength, he could not free it from the corpse's forehead before the more fearful of those looking on dissuaded him from taking further action. Albok decided not to pursue the issue at this time, but he was determined not to allow it to follow Tacquish to the grave.

Albok considered his war ax to be a prized possession. He had found it several lifetimes ago on his trek up from the southern edge of the continent to where he now found himself. It was one of a kind, the likes of which he would probably never see again. The twisted iron-wood handle had grown around the obsidian ax blade, securing it in a way that rawhide or woven cord could not. He had carefully sharpened the glassy stone into a wickedly sharp edge and broke many other implements in the process of trimming the solid wooden handle to a serviceable length. He planned to wait until he and the body were far from the village to reclaim his weapon—even if he needed to pulverize Tacquish's skull to do it.

Finally, after the warriors were chosen by draw, their first task was to wrap the body securely in deer hide. Albok volunteered to undertake this chore, seeing the rest were hesitant even to approach the corpse. Afterward, at his insistence, three of them reluctantly assisted him in lashing the body onto a makeshift sled of old goatskin. The hide, which long ago had desiccated into a stiff length of leather, was unsuitable for anything else, and hence deemed as no great loss. Two long, wooden poles extended from the front of the sled so that the warriors could transport it without touching the stiffening corpse.

The Elders were hopeful that their preparations would placate the Nukat, the elemental beings created by the Gods, Muut and Temayuwat. In their minds, only those deities could contain the immense strength of Tacquish's spirit. The man, who had been such a monster in life could be no less—even in death. During the countless years that the Shaman wielded his oppressive power over the Iviatim, few dared to whisper the unspeakable deeds attributed to him.

When Tacquish first came among the tribes, supposedly hundreds of moons before, he claimed to be a healer. However, it soon became known that his cures carried a terrible price. The villages that refused to pay his tribute suffered greatly. Those brave or foolish enough to defy him openly often disappeared or died painful and mysterious deaths. There was talk that Tacquish was more demon than man, so when maidens from many tribes began to go missing the rumors began. They said he had taken the young women not only to eat their flesh but to consume their souls. These unspeakable acts continued for many years until the coming of Albok.

When Albok arrived at the village of the two rivers, he said he belonged to one of the lake bands. The story that Albok told as he went from village to village was that he was searching for the tribe of his birth mother. As there were numerous lake bands, no one questioned this. It was a plausible tale, since stealing brides from a vanquished foe had been more commonplace many seasons ago, when the weather was foul, and food was scarce. Much had changed since then. The drought that drove many of the bands northward had finally abated. The Gods had blessed the people of the lake with fair weather and abundant game for many seasons, and now other than personal disputes there was little reason for the tribes to resort to warfare. If not for the rise of Tacquish, it was difficult to conceive a more idyllic existence. Simple and good-natured, the Iviatim people accepted Albok's explanation as he moved among them, never suspecting that his real story was far more complicated and much, much darker.

Shortly before dawn of the next day, the warriors set off with their gruesome burden to begin the two-day journey to the valley of Nukat. The trek was familiar to all of them, so they quickly acquired the well-worn trail. The tribesmen spoke little as if they feared their conversations might rouse the corpse they dragged behind them. They stopped only occasionally to relieve themselves and to drink from the underground springs they encountered on their way through the heavily overgrown woodlands.

In the late afternoon, they stopped to make camp, as sundown in the shadows of the mountains came early. They agreed that one of them should stay awake to watch over the body, which they placed well away from where the others would sleep. To everyone's relief, Albok volunteered to take the first shift.

Tending to the small fire he made for himself, Albok contemplated all that had befallen him, but most of all he thought about Tacquish's last words. Uttered with his final breath, the sibilant malediction he hissed with a twisted smile dripped with hate. The imprecation was as simple as it was chilling: "Live forever in misery."

How ironic, Albok thought in his native Greek, contemplating the dim outline of the circle under the skin of his right palm. *To suffer the same curse twice.*

CHAPTER FOUR

Los Angeles, California. Present day.

WHEN I GOT BACK to my office, the door was open, and all of my furniture was still there. So was the damn cat—fast asleep on my desk chair. I thought this could be the perfect opportunity to chuck the furry freeloader out the door. But it must have read my mind as it sprung back under the couch as soon as I got close enough to grab it.

Shit...

Just as I was pondering what it might be using for a cat box, I looked up to see one of my least favorite people in the universe knocking on the door frame. It was Detective Brent Todd. In my book, he's the one guy who can ruin a perfectly good day by simply showing up.

"Catch you at a bad time, Tonnick?" His tone wasn't the usual angry sneer I'd come to expect from him. I realized that I was still hovering over the desk chair, my arms outstretched, reaching for the cat that was no longer there.

"Not really," I answered while trying to regain my normal posture as gracefully as I could manage. "What are you doing here?" There was never much love lost between the two of us, so there was no use wasting much time on pleasantries.

He surprised me. Instead of throwing the expected insult my way he only shook his head in resignation.

"I knew this would be a mistake," he said, in a voice more weary than contentious. That got me wondering.

"If you're not here to arrest me, have a seat," I offered.

Todd didn't even try for a comeback. He merely sat down, looking every bit as tired and worn as the beaten leather couch he was

23

slouching on. In all the time I've known him, I'd never seen him like this.

"Hey, Tonnick," he sighed. "I know we've had our differences, and frankly, this might be a total waste of time for both of us, but I need your help."

I looked at him for a long moment. I guess my disbelief was spelled out in large, red capital letters all over my face.

"Okay," he mumbled as he started to rise. "I knew this wouldn't work out."

"Sit down," I said, without my usual trademark sarcasm. For Brent Todd to ask me for help was as unbelievable as Tiger Woods taking a vow of celibacy. "So, what do you need?"

"I need you to help me clear my name," he said wearily. "They've taken my badge. I'm on suspension, pending an IA investigation."

"What's the beef?" I asked as I unlocked the drawer with the Cuervo in it. Todd and I have been butting heads for a long time since he's always blamed me for the murder of his sister and her family. Little wonder, since it was my lost handgun that her husband used to commit the bloody deed. Because of that, I've never carried a gun since.

"Money has gone missing from evidence," he replied, taking the grungy shot glass I offered him. "Lots of it. It was crucial to a big-time drug case, and the DA's office is convinced I stole it."

"So, what gave them that idea?"

"They've got surveillance footage from the property room that supposedly proves I boosted the money."

"Have you seen the video?"

"Yeah. It doesn't show my face, but there's enough there to crucify me. My union rep says while it's not conclusive, it still looks real bad. Shit! I'm not even sure they believe me. Tonnick, I've got to do something… This thing is already spinning out of control."

"The union will get you an attorney. The IA will do a thorough investigation. If you're innocent, you've got nothing to worry about."

Todd shook his head. "I can't depend on Internal Affairs to get it right."

"Yeah? Why is that?"

"I'm being set up," he snapped. His weariness had given way to anger. Now he sounded more like the asshole I've always known him to be.

He caught himself and softened his tone. "Listen to me, Tonnick..." He paused for a deep breath. "Mark... I need you to get to the bottom of this. I know you. You're unconventional, but you get results." He hesitated again, probably wondering if what he was about to say was going to flatter or insult me. "Besides, you owe me. My sister trusted you once."

Yeah, and that's probably what got her killed. "So, how much money are we talking about?" I asked, eager to change the subject. I picked up a pencil from my desk. I wasn't going to write anything down, but I wanted to have something else to look at other than his accusatory stare.

"Fifty fuckin' grand. Cash, in hundred-dollar bills."

"I have to ask. Were you having money trouble? It's the first thing IA will look for."

"Not until now," Todd replied with a dismissive huff. If he thought I was bringing up that issue because I doubted his innocence, he didn't show it. "Not only am I suspended from duty without pay, but they've also frozen my checking and saving accounts! I'm living on credit cards."

The bells went off in my head. I turned my gaze away from the pencil and looked him in the eye. "So, is that why you came to me? Because you're broke?"

He returned my glare and retorted, "I'll make sure you get paid, Tonnick... Somehow."

He ran his hands through his thick brown hair. It was strange to see him so disheveled. He was one of those guys who made sure they were always impeccably dressed with every hair in place—the perfect picture of self-assured confidence. Not now though. Today, he looked like crap, and I told him so.

"Thanks... Like I didn't know! I haven't been able to sleep since this whole thing started. And to top it off, the D.A. needs the missing money to make the case stick, or the guy might walk. That's why they're going full out on me. Instead of the perp, I'll be the one doing time!" He slammed his fist on my desk in frustration. "Come on, what's it gonna be? Are you going to help me out, or what?"

I thought about it before I reluctantly replied. "Okay, I'm in. But, you've got to give me someplace to start. Did you bust the guy?"

"Hell no! Since I transferred up from the Orange County Sheriff's Department, I work robbery-homicide, not vice. I didn't even find out about the case or the money until IA showed up at my house with a warrant."

"I'm assuming they didn't find anything, or you wouldn't be sitting here," I said, refilling our empty glasses.

"I just can't figure why somebody'd frame me for this shit."

Despite what Todd was telling me, I had to assume there were only three credible possibilities. One: He was guilty. Two: Mistaken identity. Or three: Somebody needed a fall guy to take the wrap for the missing money. Maybe it's my suspicious nature, but I thought of one more.

"What were you working on lately?" I asked. "Anything unusual?"

"Nothing I can think of. We are massively overwhelmed; damn budget cuts have every one of us doubling up on our caseloads. I was working twenty-five of 'em with my team alone. Total of seventeen murders, one suicide and seven suspicious deaths."

"Any of those stand out?" I asked.

He knocked back a little more of the Cuervo before he replied. "Not really. Far as I can tell, every one of them is the same old, same old. Besides the suicide and the undetermined, it's mostly gang killings, domestic homicides, and vehicular manslaughter. Nothing unusual."

"I'd like a list of those. Also, what's the name of the dealer at the center of this mess."

"Wihelma Rivera. He supposedly runs an Ecuadorian operation that specializes in meth and murder... Not always in that order."

"Is he still locked up?"

"No, because of this mess, his lawyer got 'em released on bail. Sonofabitch put up half a million in cash."

"You know where I can find him?"

For a moment the old Todd was back. "What! Are you crazy? You won't be able to get within a mile of him. An' besides, from what I hear, you don't want fuck around with that guy."

"Hey. You want my help? Let me do shit my way. Get me the information."

"Fine, but just try not to get yourself killed before you find a way to get me off the hook."

"How much time do we have," I asked. *We? I was getting soft in my old age.*

"Not much. The IA hearing is in a week, but I'll round up all of the info for you by this afternoon."

"I'm out of town on business tomorrow, so the sooner, the better."

Todd nodded and threw back the rest of the tequila shot. He was halfway out the door when he turned around. "Thanks, Tonnick. I won't forget this."

I nodded back. *Sure.* "Don't bother closing the door," I said, still hoping the damn cat would get the hint and finally make her exit.

After I heard the downstairs lobby door slam shut, I poured myself another shot. Todd could be a jerk, and not much of a detective to boot, but I would never make him for a dirty cop. First of all, he wasn't smart enough to pull it off and lastly, he was one of those idiots that really believes in truth, justice, and the American way. I wordlessly toasted his naïveté and drained my glass.

27

CHAPTER FIVE

The Woodlands near the Cahuilla Lakes, North America. 500 B.C.

SHROUDED IN CLOUDS, THE moon god, Menily was nearly halfway across the sky when Jakem reluctantly relieved Albok from his watch. Despite the mild night air and the nearby campfire, the youthful warrior shuddered as he sat on the ground next to Albok.

"Brother, you may go and sleep now," He said in a whisper. His eyes flitted nervously from the forest floor to the hide-wrapped body of the fallen shaman.

"I will sleep here, beside you," Albok offered quietly. The younger man's relief was evident.

In the same subdued tone, Jakem hesitantly asked, "Do you believe the stories? Some say that Tacquish is really the trickster god, Taqwus, who steals the souls of the living." He motioned towards the corpse which laid among the pine needles and bracken ferns some 15 hands away. "Can it be true?"

"No," Albok replied. "The proof of that is he lies there dead. You can't kill a God."

"What if he's not dead?" Jakem muttered.

"Then," Albok replied, "I shall kill him again." With this, he leaned back against the tree behind him and closed his eyes.

It was almost dawn when Kutya'i, the wind spirit rattled the branches and leaves of the forest, rousing Albok from his dreamless slumbers. Though he had awakened instantly, it took him several moments before he realized that Jakem, who still sat beside him, was perfectly motionless. Albok reached out and touched his arm. He found it as cold as the sightless stare of the youth's eyes.

Albok leaped to his feet, attaining full situational awareness in seconds. He surveyed the surrounding forest, looking and listening closely for signs of intruders. After he determined that no threat lurked nearby, he crouched down to scrutinize the young warrior's body. There were no wounds, nor any visible reason for why such a sudden and silent death had befallen him.

Albok signaled to the others, who lay wrapped in their blankets some 50 legs away. The birdsong warning cry he uttered was one that every member of the band learned as soon as they were old enough to do so. It might be a needless precaution, as there were no overt signs of violence on Jakem's corpse, but that remained to be seen.

Albok's whistles brought the other warriors to their feet with their hunting weapons in hand. In a heartbeat, they warily accessed their surroundings before gathering around Albok. They looked questioningly at him, not comprehending at first glance what had happened. Albok motioned towards Jakem's body and then gently reached over to draw the man's eyelids down over his eyes.

Whatever had stolen the youth's life was both swift and silent. Albok was a light sleeper and was only inches away from Jakem all throughout the night. Any sound or movement would have roused him instantly. *Or would it?* The thought was unsettling, and he dismissed it more out of necessity than anything else. This was no time for speculation or doubt.

Olsm, the eldest of the group, shook his head slowly in disbelief. "This is an evil omen," he intoned softly. "This must be the work of..." He paused, hesitant to even voice the dead shaman's name, but he didn't need to finish his words. They all knew what he meant, and none, not even Albok, voiced disagreement.

"What shall we do with Jakem?" asked Gat'eel in a trembling voice. He was the youngest warrior of their number, only fourteen summers old. There were barely two years between him and his dead friend.

"If we leave him here, the spirits of the forest will take him," replied Olsm. "We have no choice. We must also carry him to the valley of Nukat, so we may honor his life."

Albok helped Gat'eel and several others in fashioning a second sled from fallen branches. They wrapped Jakem's body in the coarse blanket of his bedroll and tied the shrouded corpse to the sled with the braided rope they hastily fashioned from strips of dogwood bark. By the time the five remaining warriors resumed their journey, the sun was directly over their heads.

Several hours later, when they reached the edge of the forest, they had to abandon dragging the sleds for fear the narrow, rocky trail would quickly break the wooden poles. Hoisting the sleds onto their shoulders, the warriors bore the bodies of Tacquish and Jakem. The way was steep, and their burdens were heavy, so they worked in alternating pairs. In this fashion, the group trudged up and over the granite slabs lining the rugged foothills until the trail gave way to a sandy path that wound its way through a notch in the mountain. At the summit of that pass, they could make out the faint tracings of the game trail that led down to the valley of Nukat.

By the time they finally reached the valley floor, it was nearly dusk. Despite the lateness of the hour, Olsm directed that they begin preparing the rituals for both of the dead. The six men set about to their grim tasks, eager to be done with them before nightfall.

For Tacquish, there was little left to be done, save for interring the body. They left Gat'eel behind with Jakem's body while the rest carried the shaman's corpse into the center of the valley. Once they determined where to lay it down, Albok peeled back the stiff hide from Tacquish's head intending to retrieve his war ax. The act moved Olsm to protest in horror, but to the amazement of both men, the weapon was gone. Only the deep gash remained, and Tacquish's open and cloudy eyes seemed to mock their puzzlement. Olsm, equally angry and frightened at what Albok had done, looked away and loudly commanded him to quickly bind up the corpse again.

Meanwhile, several of the other warriors had gone to a nearby swampy meadow dotted with rocks of various sizes. Gathering the heaviest of them, they carried them back to where Tacquish lay and continued to pile them one by one over his hide-wrapped body. Albok and Olsm joined in this effort and the group continued working until the mound they had created was equal in height to the tallest of them.

The weighty heap of rocks would ensure that the ghost of the shaman would remain trapped and powerless, held fast by the elemental gods of the Earth. The Nukat, who were powerful and sometimes unpredictable spirits, would stand guard over the grave and prevent Tacquish from returning to the world in any form, human or otherwise. Or so they believed.

While this task was being accomplished, Gat'eel remained at the mouth of the valley preparing Jakem's body for the traditional cremation. Without unwrapping the body from the blankets that bound it, he gently folded the corpse into a sitting position over the large pile of dried leaves and dead wood he had gathered. Shortly after sundown, Albok and the others returned to where Gat'eel sat waiting for them.

Soon, the moonlight was glinting off the granite and sandstone canyon walls illuminating Jakem's funeral pyre in a pale glow. All the bands of the Iviatim held rituals for the dead once each year during the winter to honor death and all who had met it. It was always a six-night affair of both celebration and mourning. It would be then that Jakem's name would be added to the list of those who had gone to be with Mukat, the creator. Now however, the only concession to ceremony was a brief prayer before lighting the cairn.

Gat'eel lifted his makeshift torch from the small fire he had built next to the funeral pyre. The oily sap of the torch sputtered in the moonlight as he held it to edges of the stacked wood. The warriors stood silently watching as the dried branches and tinder burst into small, yellow gouts of flame that grew larger and larger as more of the fuel accelerated the fire into a huge roaring wall of flame and smoke. The light it cast made wild shadows that danced around the circle of men as they paid silent tribute to their fallen comrade.

As the fire consumed the blankets surrounding the body, the coarse cloth fell away to reveal the features of the man who had been placed in the traditional squatting pose. The moon and the flames now clearly illuminated the figure in the center of the conflagration. As the fire blackened and shriveled the face of the corpse, the entire group, save Albok, reacted with yells of dismay. It was plain for all to see that it was not Jakem's body that had been consigned to the fire so its spirit might be freed. It was Tacquish.

CHAPTER SIX

Los Angeles, California. Present day

IT WAS ONLY AN hour after Todd left my office that a messenger appeared with a large, brown manilla envelope and a receipt for me to sign. He hesitated after he handed it over, probably waiting for a tip until he realized I wasn't good for it. I closed the door on him as I busted the seal and emptied the contents onto my desk.

I ignored the paperwork and focused on the one piece of evidence I assumed was crucial to the prosecution's case. The thumb drive. I don't know a lot about technology, but video evidence is hard to disprove, provided it comes from a secure source. Here, from what Todd had told me, the video contents on the drive had come directly from the LAPD's own surveillance cameras. In other words—he was screwed.

I took the drive downstairs to the Cash4U Pawnshop where I badgered Willy, who owns the place, into letting me use one of the many laptops folks had cashed in for one reason or another. He watched over my shoulder as I fumbled with the thumb drive.

"Porn?" Willy asked casually. "You know it's pretty much free online."

"Good to know," I replied. "But actually, this is from a client."

Willy raised his eyebrows in mock surprise. "You gotta client?"

"Haha. Hilarious. Hey, how does this go in here?"

Willy snatched the thumb drive and deftly turned it over and inserted it in a single move. "You had it upside down," he added as he reached over and clicked some keys. "I assume you want to play the video that's on it?"

I didn't answer since the video had already begun to play. It displayed a date and a time stamp which continually updated as the video rolled. The camera was positioned overhead in the property room and aimed downward, clearly showing the logbook on the counter of the evidence cage. As soon as the guy entered the frame and signed the log, I knew it was bullshit. First of all, you couldn't see the guy's face and secondly, he was wearing a hat. That tore it for me. Anybody who knows Todd gets that the guy is a total narcissist. I've never seen him in a hat because he likes to show his headful of perfectly coiffed hair.

But there was the ring. It was prominently featured in the video as the guy checked out the box and signed the register. I recognized it immediately, and I'll bet a case of booze the watch commander did too. It was the only piece of jewelry Todd ever wore. His oversized, high school class ring.

"What's in the box?" Willy asked.

"Fifty grand in cash. Supposedly."

"They keep that kind of dough in a cardboard box? That don't make a lot of sense."

"No, Willy. Now that you mention it, it doesn't. However, that's the way they roll."

I knew from other ex-LAPD that there was an elaborate protocol in place for all cash seizures over ten grand. Right off the bat, the arresting officer has to request that the highest ranking cop available responds to the scene. Until the superior officer gets there, no one, including the arresting officer is allowed to touch or even count the money. At that point, all they can do is photograph the cash in the location where the currency was found.

Then, the AFID, the Asset Forfeiture Division, is supposed to appear on scene to collect the cash and transport the money to the station, where it's put into evidence. In this instance, the money was apparently found in the box, and it was all impounded together as evidence. After the trial, if the funds were determined to be drug-related, or illegal in any sense, the currency would be deposited into a

"Pre-seizure Checking Account." Then, all of it gets divided up between the Feds and local law enforcement. All very neat and tidy that is—unless somebody screws up.

I wondered why the officer on duty in the property room handed over the box with the cash in the first place. The answer was contained in the paperwork, which I reviewed after I returned to my office. The officer in the property room, Evan Gonzales, was a three-year veteran who, according to his deposition, wasn't aware of the box's contents. That was an oversight on his part since he didn't bother to check the description in the computer. Gonzales claimed the system wasn't working on the date and time in question. Besides, according to him, the guy who signed out the box claimed he was taking it to court. For that oversight, Gonzales was reprimanded and caught a one-week suspension without pay. It would have been worse except for one thing. He was able to pick Brent Todd out of a lineup.

I kept reading, and it got worse. The sign out on the log book was some random name and badge number, but the most damning evidence was Todd's bank account. He had evidently deposited six cash deposits over so many days around 9k apiece at different bank branch locations. Regardless of the attempt to skirt normal bank reporting, the deposits had been flagged as suspicious, nevertheless. The rest of the depositions I reviewed were mostly the prosecution doing its diligence. Judging from the discovery docs and video, it appeared they had Todd dead to rights.

I wasn't buying it. Todd wasn't the brightest lamp on the wall, but he wasn't that stupid. If he did walk out of evidence with fifty grand in cash, he sure wouldn't have deposited it into his bank account. If the IA weren't so eager to put the blame on Todd, they would have also considered that. The more I thought about it, the more the whole thing smelled. A few minutes later, things got even more interesting.

I had thrown the envelope and its contents into a desk drawer and poured myself another small shot of tequila and began running the pieces through my head when I heard footsteps coming up the stairs. The cat who had been asleep on the far corner of the couch suddenly awoke at the noise. In the next instant, it had jumped onto the floor and jetted underneath the couch. I took that as a warning and readied myself for whatever was going to happen next. Seconds later, two guys barged into my office.

One was much taller than the other, but they wore the same grim expression on their faces. I knew immediately they hadn't come to inquire about my services or anything else. I remained seated in my chair, but thanks in part to the kitty's early warning, every muscle in my body was tensed for what I sensed was coming.

Without a word, the tall guy rushed around to the back of my chair and wrapped his long arms around me, pulling me back away from my desk. Purposely, the other guy closed in, slipping on the steel knuckles he drew from his coat pocket. Plainly, they intended to pound me to a pulp.

It might have worked except for one detail. Like most of my office equipment, my swiveling desk chair has seen much better days. Several of the six wheels at its base are so loose it doesn't take much to make any of them fall off—especially when I shift my weight. That was exactly what I did as the short guy drew alongside me while the guy restraining me was turning the chair towards my attacker. Three castor wheels slipped out of their well worn holes, and the chair dipped backward abruptly. The unexpected moved made the tall guy lose his grip on my chest just as shorty drew back his arm to throw the first punch.

As the goon's fist headed for my face, I twisted and freed myself from the tall guy's grasp. At the same time, I slid out of my chair underneath shorty's punch. Instead of connecting with my face, he smashed his hand onto the back of the heavy oak chair. He yelled in surprise, recovering enough to reach out in hopes of grabbing me—but his brass knuckles made that move awkward, especially since I had already scooted underneath my desk.

The tall guy scrambled in an attempt to seize hold of me again, but he only got in his buddy's way. While the two of them became ensnared with one another, I quickly crawled out from under my desk and headed for the door. I slammed it closed behind me and hauled ass down the stairs.

I heard them follow me down, but I had already ducked into Willy's shop. He figured it out instantly from the look on my face and picked up the big baseball bat he keeps behind the counter. The two thugs halted at the bottom landing, glaring at us and contemplating their next move. However, once they saw Willy, who is nearly as wide as his six-foot height, with bat in hand, they decided to keep going. They didn't need to say anything, their expressions plainly stated they would be back.

"Tonnick. One of these days you're gonna get y'self killed," Willy wisely observed.

"Thanks, Willy. I owe you one."

"Hell, you owe me more than that! What did you do to piss those guys off?"

"I have no idea," I said innocently. But actually, I did. Someone wanted Brent Todd to go down hard, and it had been worth an investment in private muscle to make sure somebody like me didn't get in the way. That revelation got me wondering about the fifty-thousand dollars showing up in Brent Todd's bank account. "Just another day at the office," I said before I headed back upstairs.

At least now, I reasoned the drug dealer was in the clear. He'd be more interested in getting his money back than hiring a couple of guys to roust the PI who was working to clear Brent Todd. If I had to wager, I'd bet the rightful owner of the cash had jumped bail and was on his way back to South America. Everything pointed to a third party who had made a fifty-thousand dollar down payment to insure Todd was found guilty. That struck me as an expensive price tag for mere revenge. It had to be something more—but what?

Once I got back inside my office, I locked the door and got on the phone to Todd. He answered on the fourth ring. I angrily interrupted him mid-greeting. "What the hell have you gotten me into?"

"What are you talking about," he said. I had to say, the surprise in his voice was convincing. "Did Internal Affairs contact you?"

"Not unless they've taken to questioning people with brass knuckles."

"What? You're shitting me?"

"Not even a little. Two toughs just came in here and tried their best to make a piñata out of my head! I'm not working on anything else that would elicit that kind of reaction. Tell me what's really going on... Why the hell would anybody spend fifty grand to kick your ass into jail?"

"I have no goddamn idea! This whole thing is like a fucking nightmare! As if my marriage falling apart isn't bad enough."

"Are you sure that there's no big case you're working on that might be connected somehow?"

The frustration in Todd's voice was loud and clear. "No! I told you. All small time shit! None of this makes any sense!"

Gears in my head were spinning. Now, maybe it's the way my mind is wired, or perhaps I've spent too many nights peering into bedroom windows—so I asked. "You said you aren't on good terms with your wife?"

There was a long pause before Todd answered. "Yeah... You could say that..."

"What do you mean exactly?"

"A few weeks ago... She pretty much left me. She said, 'we'd grown apart.'" He stopped to take a deep breath. With a guy like Todd, it was hard to tell which upset him more. His break-up or the blow to his ego. "Last night she called to tell me she has some papers she wants me to sign. I guess she's filing for divorce... I'm hoping I can talk her out of it. We're going to meet tonight at Dillam's Grill, downtown."

"Do you think she's seeing anyone else?" I asked flatly. I can't help it. Like I said, it's a part of my process, carefully honed over years of chasing cheating spouses.

"Hell no!" Todd spat, not bothering to hide his growing agitation. "Lisa? Not in a million years!"

"Hey, calm down, Todd. I'm not trying to upset you. But it may be a missing piece of the puzzle."

"What the hell are you talking about?"

"I'm not sure. At least not yet. What time are you meeting her at Dillam's?"

"Six-thirty... Why? What are you thinking of doing?"

"Nothing. I was Just asking," I lied. I had a crazy hunch, but it wasn't worth riling him up even more. "Good luck with the wife."

"Thanks, Tonnick," he said, suddenly sounding distracted. It was doubtful he had the same idea I did. As soon as he rung off, I began planning my evening, starting with a visit to Dillam's Grill.

I had been sitting in my dilapidated Toyota since 5:30, at a reasonable distance away from the Dillam's Grill parking lot. My little Nikon pocket camera has a good optical zoom, made even better with its built-in 12X electronic boost. The position I had chosen provided a clear view of the entire lot and the restaurant's rear entrance, enhanced by the camera's viewfinder. Dillam's was a popular rendezvous spot, and I had plenty of experience trailing errant husbands and wives there. Although it was still daylight, I knew after sundown the lot would be well lit, so I was confident I'd be able to see whatever happened there.

Brent Todd arrived in his Nissan Altima and parked in the lot around 6:15. I could tell he was distracted since he showed none of the situational awareness that most cops, even off duty, routinely exercise. I knew he hadn't made me, or my trashed up Toyota since he rushed into the restaurant without bothering to look around. He had arrived early for the meetup, before his wife had. I found many photos of them both on Facebook, so I was confident I'd have no problem recognizing Lisa when I saw her. Privacy is so overrated.

Soon I discovered I was right on that account and maybe everything else. About twenty minutes later, Lisa Todd stepped out of a late model Bentley that pulled up next to the rear door of the restaurant. Obviously, she hadn't taken an Uber to the meeting. The short black dress Lisa was wearing showed off her slender figure and long legs. In light of what Todd had told me, it wasn't a big stretch to reach the conclusion she hadn't dressed up for her soon-to-be ex. Also, in addition to her small matching handbag, she was clutching a file folder, reinforcing my assumption she wasn't planning on a reconciliatory dinner. I snapped a photo of her opening the door with a thin smile on her face. Poor Todd, she was apparently looking forward to kicking him to the curb.

After she got out of the vehicle, it took off to the furthest edge of the lot and parked. Whoever was behind the wheel of the Bentley stayed there out of sight behind the dark, tinted windows. My take away was Lisa Todd had traded up in the relationship department—way up. From my experiences, affairs don't just happen overnight, so I figured it probably wasn't connected to Todd's recent legal woes. Just a sad coincidence adding insult to injury.

Only a few minutes after she entered, the rear door of the restaurant opened, and she rushed out without the file folder I had seen her go in with. The sun was setting, and the glaring lights of the parking lot had just snapped on revealing her expression. She looked mad as hell. That and the missing paperwork told me everything I needed to know. Things hadn't gone well.

Immediately, the Bentley drove over to meet her. While she got in, I snapped several pictures with my Nikon. I also got a sharp shot of the car's license plate as it roared out of the parking lot and onto Fountain Avenue. Predictably, a few minutes later, my mobile phone rang.

"Hey Tonnick," Brent began. From the way he sounded, I concluded he had started drinking when he arrived and hadn't stopped since. "My wife just tried to fuck me!"

I made no attempt to point out the irony of his statement. Instead, I asked, "What do you mean?"

"She tried to get me to sign some kind of crazy agreement. I said no fuckin' way and ripped it up!"

"What kind of agreement?"

"Shit! I'm not sure exactly… I haven't got two dimes to rub together, and she wants half of everything in a divorce."

"It's California, she'll get half of everything anyway," I replied.

"That's what I told her. She says it not good enough and won't cover any future income I might get before the divorce becomes final."

"That doesn't make any sense." I wondered if her new squeeze driving the Bentley was an attorney, looking to dot his I's and cross her T's—not to mention a few other parts of her body. "Hey man, I'm sorry to hear it's come to that."

"Yeah... Me too. I really love that woman."

I was thinking that somebody else did too. And perhaps whoever that was had enough dough to seal the deal on Lisa's divorce. If Todd were convicted and sent to jail, it would be a simple matter for any good lawyer to secure one. In California, contested divorces are granted all the time. With a felony conviction, even if the Todds had a prenup, which I seriously doubted, Lisa would end up with half of their community property in any event. I wondered why the issue of future income was even being discussed. The only reason I could think of was if Todd was convicted and later found innocent. In that scenario, he might be entitled to a payout of some kind, but that seemed pretty thin.

"Maybe we can work it out," he continued, slurring every other word.

"Todd, get a cab or call an Uber and go home," I said. "You've got enough on your plate without a DUI."

"Damnit, Tonnick, you're right. I guess you aren't such an asshole after all."

Don't jump to conclusions, I thought. The night was still young. "Thanks, Todd. I'll call you when I get back from Palm Springs."

"You're going away on vacation?" he retorted. "What the fuck?"

"It's business. I'll be in touch," I said before hanging up.

On my way home I stopped off at Walgreens and had them print a few 8x10s from my camera card. While the blackout windows of the Bentley thoroughly concealed the driver, I still had the license plate. Soon, in very short order I would have a good idea who Lisa Todd was shacking up with.

There are a ton of sites on the internet where you can track down the registered owner of an automobile for a fee. Of course, you need a computer to do that. However, since I was still twenty minutes out from Willy's, I resorted to the next best thing, which was a call to Delinda Djinn. With any luck, she would still be over at Ashton's place where there were more computers than hands to work them.

Delinda picked up on the first ring. "Yeah, Mark... What now?"

"Nice to talk to you too," I said. "I need a favor. I'm away from the office and need you to look up a license plate number on the internet for me."

"Does it have anything to do with AC&C's business?"

"Of course," I replied.

"Sure," she shot back sarcastically. "Forget it!"

"Wait!" I interjected, hoping she hadn't clicked off yet.

"Why?"

"Because it's important. And you can get the info far faster than me."

"I don't know how you ever managed to stay in business so long without learning how to use a computer."

"I have lots of other skills. I'm a people person."

Finally, after she stopped laughing, she said, "Okay. Let me see what I can do, and I'll call you back."

As I thought, it took her hardly any time at all. Fifteen minutes later my phone rang, and Delinda gave me a name and a street address. She reminded me she would pick me up early the next morning, but before I was able to ask "how early," she hung up. It was more than likely I couldn't get out the question fast enough because I was utterly tongued-tied when she told me who owned the Bentley. It belonged to Tommy Rosselli, lovingly referred to by his peers as "Tommy the Shark."

Lisa Todd sure knew how to pick them. Rosselli was arguably the most powerful crime boss in Los Angeles. Naturally, he had never been convicted of anything, but he had the dollars—and the juice—to pull off a frame on Todd. I reasoned if anyone could lop off one member of this love triangle; it was Rosselli. But why go to the trouble and expense? And why was Lisa so eager to have her soon to be ex-hubby sign a seemingly useless document? Was she afraid that Todd might win the lottery? I had a feeling that none of this would be easy to unravel. *What the hell was going here?*

Tomorrow morning, before I headed out of town, I planned to give Todd a call. Hopefully, he'd be sobered up by then, and we could prepare an intelligent way forward. If I could figure out how to tie Todd's legal jeopardy to Rosselli, not only would Todd be off the hook, but the LAPD major crimes division would owe me a big one.

I drove back to my office contemplating just how I could work it. Usually the saying, "Follow the money" leads to a solution, but in this case that wasn't going to be easy. When it came to laundering cash, there was nobody better at it than Tommy the Shark. The more I thought about it, the more puzzling it all was. I reminded myself that like every other case I had ever worked, the answer was usually right in front of my eyes. For the time being, whatever it was would have to wait until I got back.

CHAPTER SEVEN

Village of the Two Rivers, North America. 500 B.C.

THE LONG JOURNEY BACK to the village was somber but otherwise uneventful. None of the men spoke until they crested the rise above the great lake and paused at the welcome sight of the woven huts and cook fires that dotted the shoreline. It was only then that Olsm uttered a few grunts of relief before turning to Albok.

"I must let Jakem's women know about his fate."

Albok nodded. "I will tell the elders about Tacquish," he replied grimly.

The others were relieved that Albok had taken this responsibility on himself, and without further discussion, they resumed their trek down to their village.

Once they reached the edge of their settlement, Olsm outstretched his arm in front of the group, a symbolic barrier that caused them to stop. "No one must speak of anything that has passed until Albok meets with the council," he commanded. He waited until the five warriors nodded their assent before he lowered his arm. "Everyone will know soon enough," he added.

As they entered the village, Albok saw that the elders were already gathering by the large hut where they held council. From the expectant smiles on their faces, he judged they would not welcome the news he brought. Indeed, the elders waiting for them could see from the warrior's dark expressions that something was amiss.

Albok approached Costo, the leader of the elder's council while the others stood aside. Without speaking, Costo gestured for Albok to follow him and the rest of the council into his hut. It was not a request.

Once they had all entered, Costo closed the deer-hide flap behind them so none of the curious who had begun to gather could overhear.

Albok remained standing as the council seated themselves in a circle on the ground around him. He then told them about Jakem's mysterious death and the strange circumstances that had mistakenly resulted in the cremation of Tacquish. There was no mistaking the growing fear in his listener's eyes as he related the events of the past two days.

"Evil Magic!" Costo spat. "Now Tacquish's spirit is free to exact revenge!" He was looking directly at Albok.

"I don't fear the dead," Albok replied. "Neither should you."

The peal of distant thunder brought several of the council to their feet. Nishta, the eldest of the chiefs, shuffled over to where Albok stood. He thrust a weathered finger into the warrior's chest.

"He has heard you!" Nishta croaked in a voice that rattled like dry leaves. "His spirit has been set free, and he will come to eat your soul!"

"Let him try!" Albok replied defiantly, but he sensed what was coming.

Costo spoke next. "Your brashness will only anger the spirit further! None of us will be safe as long as you stay here." The other chiefs were nodding in agreement.

"For the good of our band, you must go," Costco ordered. "We will attempt to appease the spirit of Tacquish so it will seek only you."

Nishta, still standing added, "You may take only what you can carry, but you must leave now."

Albok didn't argue. That would be pointless, for unless he agreed to leave, the tribe wouldn't rest until they killed him themselves. He had no doubts that option might still appeal to some regardless of what he did. It was best to go while he had the chance. Albok harbored no regrets because eventually, he would have had to leave anyway.

Throughout his unnaturally long life, Albok had moved from place to place, village to village, to avoid the inevitable questions that would be raised should he stay in one place too long. It was the existence he had always led. Ever since the Circle of Solomon had become part of him, he had no choice. The relic from the stars beneath the skin of his right hand had made him who he was. When it granted him agelessness, it had also cursed him with an understanding that forced him to persevere in an existence that offered little reward.

His only consolation, if one could call it that, was that so many of his previous lives had become only dim memories. Otherwise, he would have gone mad with the inevitable loss of friends and loved ones over the ages. Long ago, he had decided his path was best walked alone.

These were his thoughts as he swiftly gathered his meager possessions from the woven hut that had served as his home for the past three seasons. As he wrapped them in a blanket, he thought he could hear a rising panic in the collective murmurings coming from outside his hut. No doubt the news about Tacquish was spreading among the tribe. He didn't want to see if his imaginings were true or not, so he sliced open the back of his hut and slipped into the forest.

He hadn't gotten very far before the screams reached his ears. He reacted instinctively, turning back and running towards the commotion instead of away. Perhaps this would be the day he would finally die. If so, he would embrace it. In moments, he had reached the village he had just fled. Men, women, and children were screaming in fear and scattering in all directions away from the center of the village where the apparition stood.

The horror was twice as tall as a man, and though it was man-shaped, the iridescent flames that emanated from it obscured any features it might have had. The thing was powerful, hurling gouts of fire at those fleeing in terror and plucking the limbs off any warriors brave and foolish enough to stand before it. Albok recognized Olsm in the instant before the monster tore him two.

Then, somehow alerted to his presence, the apparition paused from its murderous destruction to look directly at Albok. The flames subsided from where the being's head might have been, revealing an all too familiar face, its countenance twisted in fury and bloodlust. The hair on Albok's neck rose in a wave of disbelief. It was true. Tacquish had returned to exact his revenge.

With a roar, the fiery figure charged forward, thrusting aside anything in its path. Albok dropped his belongings and drew the blade that hung from his belt. In the same motion, he flung the knife towards the onrushing juggernaut where it struck squarely in the thing's chest. It reared up in mock surprise and anger, pulling the blade from its chest and hurled it back. Albok dodged the missile and dove to recover his weapon. He regained his feet seconds before the thing reached him, but he wasn't quick enough to avoid the impact of the monster's massive fist. The scorching blow blew him backward and knocked the knife from his hand.

With a snarl of rage, Albok regained his balance, ignoring the smoldering burn on his chest where Tacquish had struck him. Seeing his only weapon was now beyond his reach, he acted in desperation. Resigning himself to die in the next instant, Albok snatched up a nearby clay pot and threw it with all his strength. The vessel broke apart on impact with the fiery behemoth. The meager amount of water it contained evaporated in an enormous cloud of steam far out of proportion to the small volume of liquid.

As the steam enveloped him, Tacquish screamed in frustration and surprise as the flames surrounding his body diminished. Albok didn't let his astonishment deter him. Retrieving his knife, he advanced towards Tacquish. Remarkably, as Albok approached it, the apparition's form became more and more transparent, as though it was dissipating along with the steam.

"This day you may have the favor of the Gods, so savor it while you can!" Tacquish hissed before disappearing at nearly the same moment Albok reached the spot where the monster had stood. Albok stood silently, contemplating the shaman's last words. He surveyed the ruined village, now deserted except for him and the bodies of the fallen. *Favored by the Gods? Was that more unintended irony?*

He reached down and picked up a large piece of the shattered clay pot that had brought about Tacquish's demise. He recognized the distinctive pattern. The vessel had been decorated with the image of the white deer, the symbol of the goddess Pemtemweha, the protector of natural order. Not daring to think what that implied, he only stared at it for a while, and then at the disc just under the surface of his palm on which it lay. Finally, he picked up his bundle where he had dropped it and resumed his journey to destinations unknown.

CHAPTER EIGHT

Los Angeles, California. Present day.

DELINDA STARTED POUNDING ON my office door at around 8:30 AM. Did I mention I wasn't a morning person? I woke up in the same position on my worn leather couch I had assumed the night before. Bleary-eyed, I barely managed to find my way to the door, but not before I discovered that the damn cat had been sleeping beside me and that my blue, Wal-Mart, designer sports shirt was sprouting bits of gray and white fur. My feline freeloader was now sitting in my desk chair grooming herself, adorning the tattered cushion with more pieces of her discarded pelt.

I chased her off, but the sudden movement it required reminded me I was more than slightly hung over. Last night, I had intended to go back to the shabby room I was renting from Mrs. Krenzman to shower and change. Instead, I had sat at my desk drinking tequila while pondering Todd's case. I hadn't developed any more theories, but my time wasn't completely wasted as I did kill the bottle.

I opened the door and croaked a weak greeting. Delinda, in response, raised one eyebrow and shook her head as if my disheveled appearance was just what she expected. Anyway, who am I to disappoint anyone?

"You're not going like that," she declared.

"Do you have to yell?" My head was ringing.

"I'm not yelling, but I'm thinking you have a hangover."

"Great detective work, Holmes."

"Come on," she gestured towards the hallway. "I'll drive you to your apartment so you can change."

I nearly stumbled down the stairs at Delinda's heels, but I made it out to the street and over to her Benz without falling. I grabbed the handle to get in the front passenger seat, but it was already occupied.

I made a conscious effort not to sound like a guy who's been up drinking all night. "Al? How are you, buddy?"

He answered me as I slid into the back seat where I assumed more of a slouch than a sitting position.

"Great!" he replied brightly with his usual toothy grin. "I'm looking forward to the trip. Haven't been down to Palm Springs for a real long time."

"As I'm sure you know, Al has a lot of experience with Native American cultures." Delinda offered as she started the car.

"Oh, I remember you mentioning it," I muttered closing my eyes. The hazy sunshine was still bright enough to make my optical nerves scream. "One of his many past lives."

Al chuckled good-naturedly. "True enough."

It was a short trip down the block to Mrs. Krenzman's liquor store. My room was in the living space above her shop. When I got kicked out of my former lodgings a few months back, she practically demanded that I stay in her spare room. I guess she felt she owed me since I saved her and a bunch of other small business owners in the neighborhood from getting ripped off over a bogus disabled persons lawsuit.

I didn't charge any of them, considering it my civic duty to keep scumbags from victimizing folks who are scrambling to make a living. Yeah, I know what you're thinking—working for no pay is crazy, right? On most days I'd be the first to agree with that, but these folks are as close to family as I'll ever get, so they'll never see a bill.

Mrs. Krenzman was a lovely lady in her early seventies whose husband had died behind the counter—shot during a botched robbery attempt. As I trudged through the store and carefully navigated the stairs up to my room to shower and change, I tried not to look as miserable as I was feeling. From the expression on Mrs. Krenzman's face, I knew I wasn't fooling anybody.

"Too much is no good, Mr. Tonnick," she shouted up at me in her thick, Russian accent. "Maybe I no sell you no more tequila this week!"

"Now there's a good idea," Delinda concurred. She had followed me into the shop, probably to make sure I didn't pause around the aisle with the Jose Cuervo, while Al stayed in the car.

During my stint in the service, I learned how to perform the three S's —shit, shower, and shave—in quick succession, which I did, pausing only to toss a few aspirins down my throat. I'm not heavily invested in fancy clothes, nor do I own an iron, so the clothes I changed into weren't much less wrinkled than the ones I slept in. However, they were free of cat fur, a decided improvement.

I remembered my promise to call Todd, so I took a moment to punch in his number. I had no intention of sharing what I knew about Lisa's new paramour, because if I did, more likely than not, he'd do something stupid. I assumed he was still sleeping off his bender as his phone went straight to voicemail. After I left a brief message telling him I'd call back when I returned from Palm Springs, I grabbed my wallet and keys. I was still pushing them into my pants pockets as I started towards the stairs. That's when I heard all hell break loose down in the shop.

"Shut up, lady! Just put the money in the bag, and nobody gets hurt."

Peering over the narrow landing at the top of the stairs, I saw Delinda standing next to Mrs. Krenzman. She had both of her hands up while Mrs. Krenzman, looking like she could barely suppress her panic, was pulling money out of the cash drawer. She used to keep her husband's pistol in there, but I dissuaded her from doing that some time back. That was what got her husband killed.

"That's it!?" yelled one of the two guys looking at the handful of ones and fives. They were both white guys, dressed in long-sleeved hoodies pulled down low, presumably to conceal their faces. Even so, there was no mistaking the feral gleam in their eyes. They looked to be in their early twenties, and from their overall appearance, were living on the streets. There were pale blue prison tats on their exposed wrists and hands, so this wasn't their first rodeo. Both were brandishing cheap handguns leveled directly at the two women. From their body-language, I got the impression they wouldn't hesitate to use them.

"There better be more than that, or we'll kill you both," the second guy growled.

Knowing the amount of daily business Mrs. Krenzman does convinced me that unless I did something incredibly stupid, she and Delinda stood a good chance of catching a bullet. There weren't any good options—I was unarmed since I never carry, and 15 feet away—but I had one advantage. They hadn't seen me yet.

The only idea I came up with was one hell of a crazy long shot. Blame it on the residual alcohol left in my system from the night before because if I were completely sober, I would have never considered what I was contemplating. When one of the punks pulled back the hammer on his pistol, I knew it was now or never.

I leaped from the landing, grabbing hold of the giant plastic Budweiser bottle that hung from the ceiling in the center of the store. One of the two wires suspending it broke—luckily the rear one, propelling me like a monkey on a swing. I smacked forcefully into the guy who had cocked his gun, taking him by surprise. The impact made him collide into his buddy, who was likewise unprepared for my improvised intervention, knocking the pistol out of his hand.

Things weren't going as planned. The guy I crashed into still held on to his weapon and recovered his balance quickly. He whirled around and squeezed off a shot at me, which shouldn't have missed, but it did. Like an idiot, I rushed him, fast and hard before he could fire again. I drove my knee into his groin, and with a commando move I learned in Iraq, smashed him squarely in the Adam's apple as he doubled over. I made sure to strike his neck with the bony part of my hand, between the hook of my thumb and outstretched forefinger—preventing the possibility of a glancing blow. A moment later, gasping for breath and choking in pain, he dropped to the concrete floor like a felled tree.

The other guy was scrambling on his hands and knees towards the gun he dropped. I ran towards it, but I was too late. He reached it first and pointed it straight at Delinda's head. At this range, all he needed to do was fire in her general direction.

He screamed, "She's gonna die because of you, asshole!"

It's funny how during moments of extreme stress time seems to stand still. Right then, the world seemed to stop. Time itself froze, or at least some of it did. Without thinking, I threw myself between the shooter and Delinda. The punk pulled the trigger, and I braced myself for the bullet's inevitable impact, but there was only a click. His gun had misfired. The shooter's immediate reaction was to try again, but the hammer came down uselessly a second time. Panicking, he threw the gun down and ran out the door, nearly bowling over Al who was on his way in. His buddy in the meantime had struggled to his feet and wasted no time doing the same.

"I called the cops as soon as I saw them go into the store," Al said watching the would-be robbers tear down the street.

"Mr. Tonnick, are you okay?" Mrs. Krenzman asked as I reached down to pick up the would-be robber's discarded weapon.

"Sure," I replied confidently. "I don't even think it's loaded!" To illustrate my contention, I pointed the pistol straight up at the ceiling and pulled the trigger. There was a loud bang, and a shower of plaster rained down on my head. I thought I heard Delinda laugh. *No wonder why I hate the damn things!*

CHAPTER NINE

Los Angeles, California. Present day.

I WAS EXPECTING THANKS for my selfless show of heroics, but instead what I got was Delinda Djinn yelling. "What the hell did you think you were doing! Trying to get yourself and everybody else killed?"

"No," I argued defensively, "I was trying to save you!"

"Really? I didn't need saving!" Delinda retorted. "The gun wasn't going to go off!"

"How did you know that? Magic?" I protested. With a certain amount of indigence, I brushed away pieces of the plaster ceiling that had landed on my head. I was still a little shaky and was only now becoming aware of a thousand little hammers industriously using my brain as an anvil.

"What else?" Al chimed in an amused voice.

I should have seen that coming. You can't win with this crew. Still, I was grateful the punk's weapon had failed—whatever the reason.

I was searching for the right sarcastic comeback, but it caught in my throat when Delinda's expression unexpectedly softened. "Thanks anyway, Mark."

You could have knocked me over with a feather until she followed it up with a terse admonishment. "Never do that again!"

"Don't tell me what I can or can't do," I replied testily.

"Then quit acting like some macho superman," Delinda countered. "You're not!"

"Hey kids," Al interjected. "Let's take it down a notch, shall we."

I exhaled and shook my head. "Obviously, I should have just let those two guys rob the store!"

"Stop it! All of you!" Mrs. Krenzman ordered. "She right, Mr. Tonnick. It not worth no one getting hurt! Believe me, I know."

I nodded contritely. "I'm sorry, Mrs. Krenzman. You're right." There was no need to upset her further.

"Good," Mrs. Krenzman replied, happy to have made her point. "Do you think he's okay?" she added, addressing Delinda.

Delinda flashed her a confident smile. "Well, he may have hit his head, but seeing it's the hardest part of his body he'll probably be fine."

"Very funny!" I moaned.

"Don't look at me," Al said smiling. When Delinda wasn't looking, he gave me a wink as Mrs. Krenzman handed me a plastic bag full of ice.

"For your head," she explained, giving me a grandmotherly peck on the cheek.

I accepted the ice and asked if Mrs. Krenzman needed us to stay until the police arrived.

"No need. Like other times, they not come very soon." She looked down at her empty cash drawer. "And they do nothing."

I pulled a fifty-dollar bill from my wallet. "Here's a down payment for all the free sandwiches you've given me."

She held up her hand to protest, but I grabbed it and put the fifty in it. "Really, Mrs. Krenzman, it's the least I can do." She was going to argue, but I shot her one of my award-winning grins as I left, following Al and Delinda back out to the street.

When we got back to the car, Al graciously offered me the front seat. I had hardly slammed the car door shut when Delinda gunned the engine and tore down Sunset Boulevard. No one said anything until we got on the freeway. As usual, I clutched at the passenger side handgrip as she accelerated the Benz way beyond any sensible speed. I used my other hand to hold the bag of ice on my head, which had begun to ache even more than my regular self-induced hangover.

In spite of myself, I had to say it. "Damnit, Delinda! Did you have to do that?"

"Really? I don't know what you're talking about," Delinda demurred.

"I know I didn't hit my head," I sputtered. "So, why do I have a bump?"

"It's a reminder to never do anything like that again."

"I'll keep that in mind next time someone's pointing a gun at you."

"The day I need your help," Delinda retorted, "I'll…"

"Hey guys," Al interrupted. "Can we try not to argue the whole way down to Palm Springs?"

"Okay," I agreed since this conversation wasn't going anywhere fast. "Instead, why don't we discuss what the plan is once we get where we're going."

"Well, I'm sure you read the information Ashton gave you yesterday," said Delinda. I could tell from her tone of voice she knew I hadn't.

"Not yet. I didn't have a chance," I answered lamely. Actually, I never even opened the folder.

"Well, now at least you'll have something to do on the three-hour drive," she said brightly as she pulled the folder out of her door caddy and threw it onto my lap.

"Thanks," I said disingenuously, wondering how she even found it where I left it in my desk drawer. Then, I remembered I didn't recall seeing her with the folder when we left my office. Probably a copy, I thought. Although something told me that when I got back to my office, I would find the desk drawer empty. I saw Al's toothy grin in the rear-view mirror. "You're enjoying this, aren't you?"

"I can't say I'm not. You're logical to a fault. That's what makes you so good at what you do. I just have a hard time knowing why you resist believing in things outside your logical frame of reference, even when the proof is staring you in the face."

"That's because my world is about things I can see, touch and feel. I'm just not comfortable with the other stuff," I replied. "I'm sorry, but that's how I'm wired."

Al chuckled. "I get that, but you won't be able to deny the evidence of your own eyes forever."

"I think he believes, but just doesn't want to admit it," Delinda offered.

I dismissed that observation with a loud sigh and opened the folder to begin reviewing the contents. At least my head had stopped hurting, and when I felt my forehead again, the bump was gone. I looked over at Delinda who spared me a thin smile.

"You're welcome," she said.

I was grateful for the relief, but shit like this can make a guy crazy. Still, I wasn't going to give her the satisfaction of admitting there was anything magical about what had just happened. Nobody needs to remind me I'm stubborn as hell.

To say the material was dry would give it too much credit. It was hard enough to concentrate already, between Delinda's crazy driving and my confusion over recent events, but I forced myself to knuckle down. The first few pages were printed out from Wikipedia about the Cahuilla Tribe. The article stated that the members of the Cahuilla Nation originally called themselves, "Iviatim." These Native Americans had been living in the region for thousands of years, making their homes near an ancient lake before it dried up in the early 1700s.

Comprised of many bands, some which are on the verge of extinction, like the Wiewa, the Cahuilla Nation achieved official recognition from the US government in the 1870s. However, their struggles to assert rightful ownership of their lands were not without the usual bullshit.

The Spanish were the first to screw around with them, beginning with renaming the tribe which was actually composed of many bands, to the "Cahuilla." When I said it out loud, Al corrected me that despite the spelling it's pronounced, "kah-wee-ah." As it happened, the

Spaniards didn't foist that name on them out of respect, since according to the article, the contextual translation was, "heathens." However, the next paragraph had a different assertion, saying the term was actually derived from the word, "Kawi'a" in the Ivia language, meaning "master." Take your choice. Whatever the truth to that was, the friendly folks from Spain also gave the tribe an ultimatum: Either convert to Catholicism or die. You can guess how that ended up.

The article also explained that even in the present day, all the Indian Canyons in the Palm Springs area have an enormous cultural significance for all the bands, particularly one called Tahquitz Canyon. Not just for the ancient petroglyphs and stone artifacts discovered there, but for the legends surrounding the area itself. A lot of that was as you would expect, and I skimmed over the collections of folk tales and the parts that detailed sacred rocks and magical waterfalls.

After reading about pilfered rock-paintings and other ecological outrages, I found the next few pages far more interesting. These were the scans of recent newspaper clippings and printouts from various social media that documented a raft of unusual events occurring in the vicinity of the Indian Canyons and surrounding areas. Despite the stories and facebook posts about livestock thefts, animal mutilations, and random property damage, I found myself focusing on the articles and related materials regarding the rash of missing teens.

The police reports were a large part of the file. They were also better than I expected, even impressive—considering the relatively small size of the Palm Springs police department. As the newspaper articles had stated, the victims were all female, between the ages of 15 and 17. The authorities suspected kidnapping, but apparently, so far there had been no ransom demands made in any of the cases. In my experience that could mean many things—all of which ran from bad to worse.

The detectives who wrote up the cases took pains to document their efforts, covering every detail. Which, was about all they could do, considering that so far they had come up with no leads. The case summaries conveyed their frustration at their lack of progress, despite having done extensive interviews and follow-ups with all potential witnesses.

Missing person number one in the file was Janis Lomas, age 16. The local police responded to her residence after receiving a call in the early evening from her distraught parents. Janis, who was always home a half-hour after her school let out, failed to show up hours later. More ominously, calls to her mobile phone went straight to voicemail.

On a directive from Mayor Henry Carillo, the Palm Springs police immediately began their investigation. That also caught my attention. Waiving the statutory twenty-four-hour waiting period to file a Missing Persons Report was not unusual, but the Mayor's personal intervention implied that the family was politically well connected. That was intriguing but meant nothing—so far.

The report also claimed Janis had no issues or problems at home or school. Supposedly there was no boyfriend either. As far as anyone knew, there were none of the usual indications that might suggest she was a runaway. Investigators also conducted searches in and around her school—where she was last seen leaving after her sixth-period class. The community also responded swiftly. There had also been a sweep conducted by local volunteers on the very next morning after Janis was reported missing. The group had scoured a large area that included the nearby Canyonlands but had found nothing.

There were two other summaries attached to the file. The one with the earliest date concluded there was a possibility that Janis had ditched the Springs for greener, and presumably, cooler pastures. However, a hasty hand-scrawled addendum entirely dismissed that theory shortly after the second girl, Marie Bolgert, vanished under similar circumstances.

As they did with Janis's disappearance, investigators reviewed the video camera footage from the high school and other nearby sources. Per the report, all the videos showed nothing more than the girls as they exited the school gates to begin their short walks home. Neither

Janis nor Marie took the school bus as they both lived less than a mile away. Like Janis, Marie Bolgert seemed to just vanish into thin air.

Kelsey Hall was victim number three. Her parents reported her missing several hours after she hadn't returned from visiting a friend's house only a few blocks away. I thought it interesting the investigators included the notation she had gone missing in a "very upper-class neighborhood." As in the other two disappearances, numerous interviews and multiple neighborhood surveillance videos shed no light onto what had become of her.

In each of the cases, there was no ransom demand so far. When you considered all of these girls had come from well-connected families with money, that was extremely unusual—at least in my experience. In a normal kidnapping scenario, there's always a money factor— unless family was involved. That didn't seem to be the case here. If there was a link between any of the victims, it was tenuous at best. The three girls apparently were only vaguely acquainted with each other only because they all went to the same school—but their social groups were different because of their ages. Janis was 16, Marie was 15 and Kelsey was 17.

Every disappearance happened a week apart, almost to the day. That provocative detail made me think there was no coincidence here. Whoever was behind the abductions was as methodical as they were brazen. And, they couldn't have done a better job of putting the community on edge.

As you would expect, news of the missing girls had an enormous impact. After the third disappearance, rumors had spread quickly. Including the one that use of modern technology in the sacred Canyon Lands had awoken Tahquitz, freeing him to roam the land and feast on the souls of young women. There were dozens of other citizen reports attached to the crime file that were just as nuts. They ranged from alien sightings to eyewitness accounts of a ghostly Indian figure roaming the Canyons at night. Superstitious Native Americans were even hiking deep into sacred lands and placing offerings to placate Tahquitz's restive spirit.

When I joked about this out loud, Al didn't find it funny. "Don't be so quick to dismiss any of that out of hand," he countered. I started to protest, but Al cut me off. "I know you can't wrap your head around any of this stuff, but take it from me. I was there."

"What? When?" I asked, knowing I wasn't going to like the answer.

"When? A few thousand years ago, at least... Way before the Iviatim became the Cahuilla. I came north with the rest of the Aztecs after the great famine hit." He paused, waiting for me to call bullshit. I didn't take the bait. We've been through this before, and I've learned it's better to just smile, nod and listen. "In my wanderings, I lived in many of the Iviatim villages around the big lake."

"What big lake?" I asked, looking out the window at the bleak desert landscape.

Al coughed up a small laugh. "Used to be a huge body of water out here... The Salton Sea is all that's left nowadays. You can see the watermarks on the mountains if you look closely. It was there where I fought Tahquitz, or Tacquish as we called him back then. Trust me when I tell you he was one bad hombre. Known for stealing young women away from their homes, supposedly to feast on their souls."

"What kind of wine goes with that?" I quipped. Couldn't resist.

"I'm glad you find that funny," he snapped. "But his power was real... And was nothing to make fun of."

Usually, he has a much better sense of humor, but I sensed I had touched a nerve. I felt terrible about that. I like the old coot, crazy as he might be. "Come on Al, you know I like to kid around."

"Sure, but it was no laughing matter back then, take my word for it... Even the mightiest warriors of the twenty bands feared him. I was strong in those times, not like I am now... And even though I was never afraid of him, I still respected his power." He paused trying to gauge my reaction.

It was an effort, but I kept my expression neutral. Despite my skepticism, I refrained from further comment, mainly since this was plainly a delicate subject. As he continued, I tried to picture Al in his prime. It wasn't easy.

"Solomon's Circles couldn't stop the aging process completely. But, in those days I had a lot more meat on these bones. I was a seasoned warrior, and as you would say now, I kicked ass! Matter of fact, I was the one who finally killed Tacquish... Or at least I thought I did."

"Yeah? What do you mean, 'thought you did?'"

"It's a long story, but if anybody could cheat death, Tacquish could... And for a little while, he did. It was only by the grace of the gods that he was banished from the realm of man."

What could you say to that? I did my best not to sound dismissive. "Well, I think it's safe to assume he's still dead."

Al shook his head. Apparently, he had given up trying to convince me. "You'd better hope so."

I took his response at face value, which was only fair since I had given up trying to imagine Al as a bad-ass Native American warrior. Now that the conversation was over, I turned my attention back to the final pages in the brief. Evidently, Ashton had saved the juiciest parts for last. These reports and photographs detailed the mutilations reported during the same period as the girl's disappearances. Three goats, four chickens, and one cow were found sliced open, their internal organs set out in a neat pile beside their carcasses.

In contrast to the detailed missing persons investigations, the police reports in these instances were notably sparse. No clues, no apparent motive, no suspects, and from what I could infer from reading between the lines, little interest. Then, I got to the very last page—the elephant in the room, and the reason for our visit.

It was an editorial cut out of the Palm Springs Times, the local newspaper, written by one Harry Chavez, a member of the Wiewa Tribal Council. In it, he unequivocally states that AC&C's recent operations were solely responsible for awakening Tahquitz's spirit and bringing him back to wreak his evil on the land. Six paragraphs later, after blaming AC&C for everything—including an acne outbreak— Chavez concludes that the company should have its wireless franchise revoked and cease doing business in the area. The cynic in me couldn't help but wonder which one of Ashton's competitors was pay-rolling this guy.

I closed the folder and tried to process everything I'd read. I didn't really give a damn about the mutilations or spirit sightings; I was thinking about the missing girls. In my opinion, the timeline didn't hold much promise for a happy ending.

It had been almost three weeks since Janis Lomas, the first victim had gone missing, and the odds were slim she was going to turn up alive. I wasn't holding out much hope for the others either. If the motive wasn't about ransom, then perhaps it was something more personal. That was a long shot, but I liked it a lot more than the soul feasting angle. A whole lot more.

CHAPTER TEN

Palm Springs, California. Present Day.

AN HOUR AND A half after I finished going through the paperwork, we finally arrived in Palm Springs. The last time I visited here was when I was eight years old, vacationing with my parents. My recollections are mainly Frank Sinatra playing on the radio and the unremitting heat. Today, the place was still as hot as I remember it— perhaps even hotter. And I guessed with street names like Frank Sinatra Drive and Bing Crosby Parkway, I'd be hearing Old Blue-eye's voice sooner than later.

The thermometer on the dash of the Benz read one hundred twenty degrees. The climate was reminiscent of Bagdad, another of my least favorite places. Considering it was just before 6:00 in the evening when we arrived downtown, I could only guess how hot it would be during the day tomorrow. That's when Ashton had arranged for us to venture out with Dr. Howard Schwartz, the archeologist. We'd know soon enough if the story about AC&C's errant cable was true or not.

We were booked into one of Palm Springs's most exclusive hotels, the Rocktide, for the duration of our stay. Ashton, in his usual classy style, had popped for the best accommodations in town. Even though I had a sneaky suspicion his company probably owned it, the place was pure swank.

As soon as we checked in, a puffy-faced kid at the desk informed us we had a reservation for dinner in the Topaz Room, an exclusive eatery at the top of the twelve-story building. This was going to be nice. All the benefits of an expense account without the paperwork. Not that I pad those, anyway. Okay—maybe just a little.

A few minutes later we were all seated at a window-side table with a lovely view of rocks, cactus, and desert-style urban sprawl. From this perch, I realized the city of Palm Springs wasn't the quaint little berg I remember from years ago. However, not everything had changed— the music playing softly in the restaurant's background was Frank Sinatra singing, "My Way."

"What are you having?" Al asked, distracting me from my not-so-fond childhood memories.

"Steak," I said without even looking at the menu. "And a double martini."

"The most expensive item on the menu, no doubt," Delinda smirked, though not unkindly.

"Hey... I never look a gift horse in the mouth," I replied brightly. "Besides, I can't even pronounce half of the entrees."

"Mark, you never cease to amaze me," Al said. "Don't you know what a steady diet of red meat and alcohol does to your arteries?"

I laughed. "Hey, some of us don't get to live forever."

Al didn't see the humor, or if he did, he ignored it. His reply was also more serious than I expected. "Take my word for it, one lifetime is enough for anybody. My head is full of things I can't forget, as much as I'd like to. Solomon's circle was no blessing." He motioned with his prosthesis. "Glad to finally be rid of it."

I guess Al has a right to be a bit touchy on that subject. The first case I undertook with AC&C nearly killed all of us, and ultimately cost Al his hand, along with the Circle of Solomon embedded in his palm. While I have no idea whether it made him immortal like he says, a madman sliced it off, nevertheless. Now Al's eventually headed for the graveyard like the rest of us. "Sorry, Al. I meant no offense."

"None taken. I'll make the most of the years remaining to me." He smiled and added, "But if you keep eating and drinking like you do, you won't have many of them left."

"It's not when you go," I quipped. "It's how you go."

"You're an ass," Delinda said shaking her head.

Thankfully, by then my martini arrived, giving me the opportunity to pretend that I didn't hear her comment—not that I let it get under my skin. She and I have this thing going, well at least I do. I pulled the olives out of my short martini and silently lamented my one-sided love affair with a woman who is utterly convinced she's a genie.

"Want an olive?" I asked, holding out the toothpick. Any decent bartender knows you put cucumber into a Hendricks martini.

"No, I don't want your olive," Delinda said sharply, waving me off. "Especially after it's been swimming in alcohol."

"Suit yourself." I'll have to take consolation in the fact that I have better taste in cocktails than in women. Which leads me to another question. Why is it I always want what I can't have? One day I'll figure that out.

"So what did you think of the brief?" asked Al getting right to the point while taking me away from my musings. I couldn't blame him for not wanting to waste any more time on pointless discussions about my health.

I took another sip of my drink before I replied. "Well, the police reports are very complete. It seems the locals have spared no efforts, but they've still come up dry. No clues, no girls, no motives, and no suspects."

"The official reports don't mention Tahquitz, I imagine," Delinda offered.

"Actually, there was one scathing editorial that brought him up while laying the blame at AC&C's doorstep. It sounded like a hit piece to me."

Al's short laugh sounded more like a dry cough. "I will say one thing, if his spirit has returned, he'll want to revenge himself on the descendants of all the tribal bands…" Al shot a glance at Delinda before he added, "Back in the day, I was strong enough to defeat his physical form, but I was no match for his spirit magic!"

He might have been in better shape a few thousand years back, but nowadays Al was as skinny as a flagpole, and his arms resembled the toothpick I had just pulled out of my drink. A strong desert wind would pick him up and send him flying like a tumbleweed. I held my tongue, but I'm sure my expression gave me away.

Al shook his head in resignation and gave me a wan smile. "Mark, I know you still don't buy into any of this, but I was real formidable back then. Hundreds of years after I left the Roman Empire in Asia Minor, my search to recapture the Talisman of Apophis led me here. Back then, this land wasn't desert... There was plenty of water and game was plentiful. Most of the tribes lived in peace during those years."

He stopped for a moment and got that far-away look folks get when they're reflecting on the past. "When I was here, I went by my Greek name, Albok. I kept to myself, as I always did, roaming around from village to village to hide the fact I didn't age. One year when the Talisman took flight once more, I fell afoul of Tacquish. He challenged me to combat, assuming that like the rest of the tribe, I was inexperienced in battle. Hell, after the Peloponnesian Wars, there wasn't much I didn't know about fighting hand to hand. So, we faced off with the rest of my band looking on... And I killed him... Or at least I thought I did."

I knew about the legend of the Talisman. The search for that cursed object was a big part of the reason Al lost his hand. "Huh? What do you mean, 'you thought you did?'" I took a long pull from my martini before I added, "Supposing what you're saying is true."

Al ignored my aside and continued without missing a beat. "I meant exactly that. Tacquish's magic was strong, even after death. When his body was mistakenly cremated, his spirit became free and returned to seek his vengeance." He shook his head when he saw my expression. "It's true. And I also wasn't exaggerating when I said it took help from one of the Iviatim gods to send him back to the spirit realm."

I knocked back the rest of my drink. "So, what you're telling me is that he could come back... Even now?"

"I am," Al replied. "However, I'm of the opinion it would take a lot more than just a little electricity to make that happen."

"So, Delinda, what do you think?" I asked. Of course, I posed the loaded question intentionally, perversely thinking she would add more mumbo-jumbo to the conversation. It takes so little to amuse me.

"I think we need to look at all explanations," she said as her salad arrived. "Both supernatural and mundane."

Her rational reaction surprised and impressed me although I had to admit I was a little disappointed that the conversation didn't veer into crazy-land. "Okay," I agreed, slicing into my perfectly cooked fillet. "First things first. What's the plan for tomorrow?"

Delinda finished a mouthful her salad before she answered. "We're meeting Dr. Howard Schwartz about ten miles from here, at 7:30 in the morning. He's going to take us to where he found the buried cable."

I'm not a big fan of early starts, but at the least, the temperature would be cooler at that time of day. She probably expected me to complain, but instead, I brought up another point. "Also, when we get an opportunity, I'd like to have another conversation with our Mr. Knowle. I believe he might know more than he's telling."

"I think you're right," Delinda said, pleased at eliciting my expression of shocked disbelief. If you haven't figured it out yet, we are rarely on the same page.

"You do?"

I know she heard the confusion in my two-word reply, but she only nodded and gave me that smile of hers—the one that drives me crazy. With her, you just can't win.

CHAPTER ELEVEN

Canyon Lands near Palm Springs, California. Present Day

THE CANYONLANDS ARE OUTSIDE the Palm Springs city limits and are, for the most part, on protected Federal or Native American reservation lands. If heat-stroke is your thing, several of the canyons are open to the public year round for hiking or other related activities. Access to other, culturally sensitive areas is allowed only with authorization from the Tribe or the Feds.

Dr. Howard Schwartz and his team were excavating near a place called Tachevah Canyon, most of which remains off-limits to the public. When we arrived the following day at our agreed on meeting point, I could see why. This was not any place to take the kids for a picnic.

The terrain was rugged and bleak, reminding me of places in the middle east I'd rather forget. I had the expectation we were all going to hike in, and Delinda, myself, and Al had dressed as Schwartz had recommended. Well, mostly, as my version of sturdy walking shoes were a pair of well-worn sneakers, since that was all I brought. I pulled my socks up over the cuffs of my lightweight long pants to keep the bugs out, and I wore a long-sleeved shirt for protection from the sun and the twisted, dried brush. I hoped the Dodger's baseball hat I wore would be enough to shield my thinning hair from the desert sun.

Delinda and Al wore hiking boots and much better headgear with wider brims. I thought that was a wise decision on their part and made me realize the tops of my ears would probably be smoldering ash by the end of the day. Schwartz was already waiting for us at the

75

pre-arranged location looking like he had just stepped out of an Indiana Jones movie.

"Are you all ready to go?" Schwartz asked jovially.

"Lead on," I replied casting an eye on the road-weary Jeep he had driven up in. There was also an old pickup with a horse trailer parked nearby.

"This way then," he replied walking away from where we parked. We followed and began what I assumed would be a long hike in the bright early morning sunshine.

The trail, if you could call it that, was a thin scar in the desert loam that stood apart from the ground around it by virtue of faint footprints and the trampled remnants of dried tumbleweeds. We followed Schwartz for about twenty minutes until we rounded a bend in the trail and came upon a group of horses tied to several stakes in the ground. An attractive girl with dark hair stood nearby, patiently waiting for us. She wore khaki shorts, and a collared long-sleeve shirt, the same as Schwartz did. However, what caught my attention was that she avoided making eye-contact with any of us. Long experience has always led me to believe that type of mannerism is a tell. One that means, more times than not, that a person is hiding something. I made a mental note to have a conversation with her later on. In hindsight, that was a mistake on my part.

"This is Meena," Schwartz said taking the reins she handed to him. "She's one of my interns."

"Welcome," Meena said. She returned the greeting in a confident voice with only a trace of a Hispanic accent. Even so, I thought she was looking everywhere else except at the three of us. "I hope you all know how to ride. Our dig is a few miles up."

"No problem," said Al. Delinda nodded in agreement. Suddenly everyone was looking at me.

"I'm good," I lied. The truth was, the only time in my life I had ever ridden a horse was when I was about 6 years old at the Griffith Park stables. At a walk. And, if memory serves, I was terrified. Nevertheless, I gamely struggled up into the saddle and prepared myself for the worst. Fortunately, the ride up the canyon was uneventful if you consider I was clinging onto the saddle horn for dear life. However, my horse knew the way, and it required little effort on my part to steer—or brake.

We followed the canyon trail quite a ways up the mountain before Schwartz and Meena slowed our makeshift caravan to a halt. "We have to go the rest of the way on foot," Schwartz explained as he deftly dismounted from his horse.

It didn't go nearly as well for me. My foot got hung up in the stirrup, and I almost broke an ankle getting back onto the ground. I'm sure the horse was just as happy as I was that the ride was over.

Meena stayed behind with the horses as the three of us followed Schwartz onto another path. This route was far too narrow for the horses to navigate. I tried not to look down the steep, switchbacked trail as we continued to trek upward on the side of the canyon wall. Finally, we crested over the top of the ridge and descended into a shallow valley.

"Here's where we found the cable," Schwartz proclaimed with a hand gesture, not unlike a ringmaster introducing the high-wire act. "We had found several artifacts in this general area before we uncovered it."

Our eyes followed his outstretched hand to a partially excavated stretch of sandy ground. The exposed portion of what appeared to be an electrical cable was as thick as my wrist and sheathed in gray rubber with the AC&C brand logo printed in a repeating pattern every few inches.

Al kneeled down to examine it closer. "Well, well. Seems to be a length of cable all right. An' the branding is unmistakable." He looked up at Delinda and me as though we might have something to add.

"Why here?" I asked. My talents don't extend to technology of any kind, but I was thinking about what it would take to string a presumably long length of cable though terrain as rugged as this. "How far does it go?"

Schwartz scratched his head, "Dunno, as soon as we found it, I passed the word to the Tribal Council. Since it belongs to you and the Feds, we didn't want to screw with it. They told us to stop digging until they could get you out here to tell us what was going on. Naturally, we tried to keep this discovery quiet but unfortunately, word leaked out before anyway."

"Who exactly found it?" I asked, although I already had a good idea.

"Meena did," Schwartz replied. "She was staking out the area... That's what we do before we begin an excavation, divide the ground into squares so we can document the dig by columns and rows. She hit the cable when she pounded in one of the stakes... That's how we found it."

"Well, quite frankly I think it's a fake," Delinda said. "I don't believe it's an active cable."

"Oh, really?" I said. "How would you know?"

She merely smiled, and Al nodded in agreement. I hate it when they do that.

"One way to make sure though," said Al. "Let's dig it out." He reached for one of the shovels lying against a nearby rock. Then, he grabbed a second one and handed it to me. "I got this end, you get the other."

"Dig, in his heat?" I knew my protest would get me nowhere—and I was right.

The two of us began digging, trenching around the cable at opposite ends of its exposed length. Under the thin layer of sand and gravel, the earth was soft. That was telling in itself. The cable hadn't been buried here that long ago. Still, it was slow going.

An hour later, I was still uncovering cable, when Al yelled, "Look at this!"

I turned to see that even with his prosthetic hand, he had dug out twice as much cable as I had. Not only that, but levered up on his shovel tip was the neatly cut end of the cable.

"Damn!" I exclaimed, amazed more at how much Al had accomplished compared to my own efforts, than by the fact that they both had been right. The cable went nowhere.

"Well, I'll be!" stammered Schwartz. "It's not connected to anything. What about the other end?"

Everybody was looking at me. I cleared my throat. "Ah, I'm not done yet."

"Let me give you a hand," Al offered with a sly edge in his voice. Delinda just shook her head.

Ten minutes later Al and I finished digging up the other end of the cable. It was also connected to nothing. All in all, the cable ran about one hundred feet from one end to the other.

"Somebody put this here hoping you would find it," I said. "It's a total fake." I was pissed. More about having to dig out a bullshit cable in the hot sun than anything else.

"Why? Just to spook the locals?" said Schwartz realizing he had been played.

"Don't you think?" Delinda replied. "It sure seemed to work!"

A question popped into my head at that moment. I turned to Schwartz and asked it. "Did Meena pick this spot at your direction?"

"No, she selected it herself. But that's not unusual. A lot of the interns I work with do the same. It's part of their job."

"How many interns do you work with?" Delinda asked.

"Depends on the time of year. Now, I have four graduate students, including Meena, enrolled in the program. They get course credit for six weeks of fieldwork."

"I think we need to talk to her," I suggested.

Schwartz nodded in agreement without replying. He had a strange look in his eyes that led me to wonder if he was really angry or merely annoyed at being Meena's patsy. Strangely and without a word of warning, Schwartz started down the canyon trail.

"Hey," I called after him. "Wait for us!"

"Let him go," said Al. "He's probably got a lot to say to her before we get there."

"I'll bet," I replied.

We followed the canyon trail back to where we had left Meena and the horses. When we drew closer, we saw only Schwartz was there waiting for us. He looked very distracted or disoriented, I couldn't tell which. I supposed he was still processing his intern's betrayal. As it was, it was a long moment before he even noticed our presence.

"I'm sorry," he apologized. "I've been out in the sun too long."

"Where did she go?" I asked. "Where are the horses?"

"I don't know," Schwartz mumbled, acting as if he had just become aware of the situation. "I don't get it. She's always been very reliable."

"I'll bet," I muttered under my breath. This whole thing was starting to smell, even worse than the horse sweat clinging to my clothes.

Suddenly, there was a loud sound from nearby. I'm no expert, but it sounded like the hooting of an owl. I was startled enough to take a quick step backward, an act that possibly saved my life. Out of nowhere, the sand erupted where I had stood a moment before. This time it was followed by an echo that sounded like a faraway handclap, a sound I recognized all too well. *Gunfire!*

"Take cover!" I shouted, and we all scattered in different directions. I crouched down behind a boulder and tried to steal a peek around it to see where the shooter might be. For my trouble, I was sprayed with slivers of exploding granite followed by another dull *crack* off in the distance.

The shooter apparently had a scope. From the delay between impact and sound I figured they were at least a hundred yards away. Apparently, whoever was firing at us was an experienced sniper. All of that was running through my head as I backed up and stumbled over something on the ground behind me. It was Meena. She was dead, her eyes still wide open in surprise.

It didn't take a genius to figure out the cause of death. Buried deep in her forehead was the business end of what looked like a Native American war ax. The wicked leading edge of the sharp, obsidian blade had been driven into Meena's skull with what appeared to be a single, powerful blow. Whoever killed her had struck swiftly and without warning, and as far as I could tell, there was no indication she fought back.

"I found Meena... She's dead!" I yelled.

In reply, more pieces of rock flew off of the boulder sheltering me, followed by the echos of the rifle shot. I pulled out my cellphone and started to punch 911. I stopped when I saw the screen read, "no service."

"What!" screamed Schwartz from wherever he was hiding. "Dead? Are you sure?"

"Yes!" I didn't need to double check. "Murdered," I shouted back. No one replied. "Does anybody's cell phone work?"

"Not up here..." Swartz's answer was cut off by the sound of even more gunfire, closer and louder than before.

These shots sounded like they were now coming from behind us. My first thought was that the shooter had circled around to close in for the kill. Seconds later, several faraway shots resumed from the opposite direction. Presumably, the sniper who had us pinned down assumed we were firing back.

The long-range shots were answered with a barrage of return fire coming from behind us, which I recognized as rounds from a semi-automatic rifle. Maybe Schwartz had stashed some protection nearby. One could only hope, although as far as I was aware, none of us had brought any ordinance like that.

Long minutes later there was silence. Then I heard Delinda's voice. "They're gone," she pronounced.

"How the hell do you know?" I said, still crouching behind the rock.

"I just do," she replied. "Absolutely positive."

"Of course you are," I muttered under my breath. Then, loud enough for all to hear I asked, "Who was firing back at 'em? You, Schwartz?"

I cautiously looked around the boulder, keeping low and ready to dive back for cover again at the slightest provocation.

"I thought it was one of you," said Schwartz as he stood up from the rock he had used for cover, only a few yards behind me.

Al had flattened himself on the ground behind a stunted Yucca plant nearby. He regained his feet and dusted himself off. "Not me," he said clearing his throat. "But, I'm grateful to whoever it was."

Schwartz and I were both staring at Delinda. She was standing out in the open, midway between where Al and I were. I wondered where she had taken cover—or if she even had bothered.

"They seemed to have been shooting at you, Tonnick," she noted dryly.

"What gives you that Idea?" I replied.

"Because just about every shot fired was aimed at the rock you were hiding behind," added Al, making it sound as if it were the most obvious thing in the world.

Delinda came over to where I remained hunkered down behind the boulder. I've been with her in a few gory crime scenes, so it surprised me when I heard her inhale sharply as her eyes fell on Meena's corpse.

"Oh my god!" Schwartz said as he joined us. He kneeled beside Meena, his face twisted in a mixture of horror and grief. "Who would do this? Christ almighty!" Then his attention became focused on the improbable cause of her death. "This war ax is an Iviatim weapon... It must be a replica... It looks brand new."

"From the expression on her face, it looks like she never saw it coming," Al remarked as he joined us. His own expression was just as unexpected. He looked like he had just seen a ghost.

"Thank God for that." Schwartz agreed in a hoarse whisper.

"Everybody okay?" boomed a new voice. We all turned to see a burly, bearded man walk up to where we were gathered. I judged him to be in his late sixties from his sun damaged complexion, which was even worse than Al's—if such a thing were even possible. The backpack he was wearing looked to be as full and as well-used as he was. He was also carrying an AR type automatic weapon slung over his shoulder.

The stranger's voice was thick and phlegmy, as though he hadn't spoken for a long time. He coughed loudly and spat out a thick wad of something I regretted seeing as he began to explain. "I was up on the rise and heard shots. I thought some bugger was shootin' at me, so I started shootin' back!"

"Did you see the guy?" I asked, finally getting to my feet. I was positive that this guy wasn't the one shooting at us. Otherwise, we would have all been dead already.

The man shook his head and pointed in the opposite direction from which he had come. "Nah, didn't see nobody. I thought maybe I saw just the glint of a scope up on the hill over yonder. That's what I was aimin' at when..." He stopped talking as his eyes fell on Meena's body. "Shit. That ain't no gunshot wound."

"No," I said. "But I've got Vegas odds on whoever did this was the same asshole that was shooting at us."

His gaze never left the girl's corpse. "Damn... Poor thing. So young," he pronounced slowly. He said it in a way that struck me as more than a little creepy. There was a moment of uncomfortable silence before Al cleared his throat.

"I think we owe you our lives," he said. "I'm Al Klepios." He gestured towards each one of us as he continued. "This here's Delinda Djinn, Mark Tonnick, and Dr. Howard Schwartz... An' you are?"

"Anders... Terry Anders. Hell, you don't owe me nothin'. I thought that sommofabitch was trying to kill me t' steal my gold! Didn't see you folks until after all the shootin' stopped." He tightened his grip on the weapon and paused to look us over before he added, "You better not be thinkin' of takin' my gold either!"

A little voice in my head decided me that Ander's brain wasn't firing on all cylinders—so I thought it best to speak up before he turned his AR in our direction. "We're not looking for any gold. We're digging for artifacts... Just old Indian stuff."

Delinda evidently caught the same drift. "Mr. Anders, we're all very grateful that you came along when you did." Her soothing tone and warm smile worked like magic to quell the paranoid gleam in Anders' eyes.

He shook his head. "Still don't know how the fuck I got here!" Ander's face reddened as he noted Delinda's raised eyebrow. "'Cuse the cussin' Ma'am. Ain't been around decent folk for a real long time. But I'm kinda confused. See, one minute I'm walking down in the shade of the canyon and the next thing I know, I'm standing on the top of the rise, thinkin' I'm bein' shot at! Funny thing... I don't have the foggiest idea of how I got there... Or here for that matter... Damnest thing!"

I shot a glance at Delinda who had her poker face on. It's funny how she makes me think she's responsible for every unimaginable event that happens to us without even a single word. Regardless, at this moment I was happy for Anders appearance, magical or otherwise. What had started out as a simple "have a look around" excursion had turned into something far more than anyone had bargained for.

Our only lucky break, if you can call it that, was that the horses hadn't wandered very far. Anders helped Schwartz track them down with the skill of someone who's lived out in the desert for far too long, at least by my reckoning. We parted company with him shortly after that. He was eager to return to the canyons before anyone could question him about his prospecting on reservation land.

"I don't think he's too long for this world," Al said as we watched Anders wander back up the trail. "Because, from the look of his face, he's using mercury to sweat the gold out of the rocks. That will kill him eventually. I'll bet he's about ten years younger than he looks."

"Look who's talking," I said quietly under my breath. While Al and I were speaking, Schwartz had gently placed Meena's body across the front of his horse's saddle. With some effort, he pulled the tomahawk free from her forehead before wrapping the bloody thing up in a canvas square and placing it in his knapsack. The guys working homicide would grind his ass down for that, but it was pointless to bring it up now.

As Al helped me get onto my horse, I asked him, "Hey... Back there, when we found the body, you looked like you had just seen a ghost. Am I right about that?"

"I might have," he admitted. "That war ax. I had one just like it a long time ago. Same ironwood handle, same obsidian blade."

"When was that?" I replied, struggling to put my feet in the stirrups.

"Many lifetimes ago," Al said seriously.

"You know that's impossible. The wooden handle would have rotted away. Like Schwartz said, it looked brand new."

Al drew his horse near to mine and spoke softly, so only I could hear. "It was burned with Tacquish's body. It was stuck in his forehead, same as it was in her's, the last time I saw it."

Despite the stifling heat, I shuddered involuntarily. Unwilling to agree with him out loud, I only nodded my acknowledgment. However, I found it impossible to contain myself any longer—I had to ask. "So, are you saying this Tahquitz guy has really come back from the dead?"

Al shrugged and gave me a look that mirrored his uncertainty. "Hell, I can't say for sure. But you have to admit, things are getting weird."

If something strikes Al as being weird, it utterly redefines the word. Although, that led me to ask another, more mundane question. "So then, why does the newly resurrected spirit of a powerful and ancient medicine man need to take potshots with a sniper's rifle?"

"I have no clue. Maybe 'cause he left his war ax somewhere," Al replied. *Now, who was being sarcastic?*

"Well, things look much less supernatural from that perspective," I said. "I'm sure there's also a reasonable explanation for the tomahawk."

"We'll see, won't we?" he countered.

"We certainly will," I said with more conviction than I felt.

"By the way," Al said, "only the Algonquians called it a tomahawk. The Iviatim called it something I'm sure you wouldn't be able to pronounce."

85

"I'm sure you're right."

Aside from my brief exchange with Al, no one else spoke on our ride back to the cars. Even though my backside was killing me, I ran all the recent events through my mind looking for the barest connection between the discovery of the cable, the recent rash of disappearances, unexplained phenomena, and now, Meena's death.

Some pieces of the puzzle were fitting together better than others. For example, I could see why Meena was murdered; presumably to keep her from revealing who set up the phony cable thing. And, it was highly probable she helped to leak the discovery too. The rumors that AC&C's tech was behind the return of Tahquitz and other supposed supernatural events surely didn't start by themselves. All of which led me to wonder about who would stand to gain from all of this. What would be worth killing for? And, how did the missing girls figure into all of this?

Once we reached the cars, Schwartz called 911 and breathlessly told the dispatcher what had happened. While he did that, I carefully got off my horse—this time without tangling myself in the stirrups as Delinda walked up.

"Mark, a penny for your thoughts?"

"Only a penny?" I joked, looking into her unbelievably green eyes. A guy could find himself lost in them.

"Really? A girl is dead, and you joke?"

"I'm sorry, you're right," I apologized. "But, it seems perfectly clear to me Meena was complicit in the phony cable scheme. She was probably killed to make sure she couldn't reveal who put her up to it. What I can't figure out is why they were shooting at us."

"Shooting at you," Delinda corrected.

"Fine. Shooting at me. Still doesn't fit. We already knew the cable was a fake, so after making sure that Meena was out of the picture why stick around to take potshots at me?"

"Well, maybe you know more than you think you do," she said smugly.

"That makes no sense," I countered. "What could that possibly be?"

"I'm sure you'll find out soon enough. You always do."

I had no answer for that, but I was warmed by her confidence and only wished I felt the same way.

About twenty minutes later a San Bernardino Police car pulled up, followed by the Palm Springs coroner's van. It took another hour to get our statements while they bagged and tagged the body. As I thought, the homicide guys were peeved at Schwartz for contaminating the murder weapon. In the grand scheme of things, I didn't think it would make any difference. The twisted wooden handle wasn't going to yield much in the way of fingerprints.

It had grown late in the day, and now that my adrenalin had simmered down I had become more aware of the sweltering heat. I was grateful to get back into Delinda's air-conditioned Benz. On the drive back to the hotel, we discussed several ideas, including who would benefit if AC&C were to lose its wireless franchise. That conversation proved to be fruitless as there were too many competitors to consider. Without some input from Ashton, it was useless to speculate.

When I finally back to my hotel room, I had planned to plunder the mini-bar, but the message light was blinking on the phone. My first thought was that perhaps Brent Todd, failing to reach my mobile had managed to track me down. It took me way too many button presses and several tries before I finally got the goddamn voicemail to playback. Another reminder that technology is not my friend.

It wasn't Todd. The metallic voice was reedy, with a thick Hispanic accent. There was no greeting—whoever it was got straight to the point. "Mr. Tonnick, I know where the missing girls are. Come alone at eleven tonight to the corner of Sinatra and Royce. I'll meet you there."

Great. If that doesn't sound like a trap, I don't know what does. Naturally, I'm in.

CHAPTER TWELVE

Palm Springs, California. Present Day.

DESPITE SHOWERING THOROUGHLY, I could still smell horse, so after I shaved, I showered again. Finally fit for company, I joined Al and Delinda at the same restaurant we ate at the night before. As I sat down, Delinda gave me a look that reminded me of the time I was tardy for homeroom in the 7th grade. I blamed my lateness on the horse smell's resistance to soap and water without bothering to mention the voice-mail I'd received.

"You're absolutely not going alone," she announced as soon as I was done making excuses.

"What? Why?" I pretended to not know what she was talking about, while at the same time hoping the surprise wasn't evident on my face.

"You know what I mean," she said sharply. "It's obviously a trap."

"Of course it is. That's why I've got to show up. By the way, are you tapping my phone?"

"Don't be so clueless. I don't need to tap your phone. I have other ways."

"Let me guess, magic?"

Before she had a chance to reply the waiter showed up with two glasses of water and a double martini. I was impressed.

"Thanks for reading my mind," I said.

"No magic involved there, I assure you." Delinda smiled. "In many ways, you are like an open book."

"Well, in that case, you know why I've got to keep that appointment."

"That's crazy. It would be suicide."

"What do you propose?"

"Don't go."

"Sorry, I've got to take the chance. Lives are at stake."

"That's not why we came down here..." Delinda objected.

"I disagree. Folks are blaming the girl's disappearances on AC&C's cable, I absolutely have to look into it."

"He's right," Al interjected. "You'll just have to look after him, Delinda."

I almost choked on my drink. "I don't need babysitting. I'm a big boy! Besides, there's no reason to put yourself in danger too."

Delinda rolled her eyes and shook her head. "You're an idiot!" She got up and left the booth and stalked out of the restaurant without even looking back.

I turned to Al. "What's her problem?"

He was smiling as he shook his head. "You are an idiot. Can't you see she's worried about you?"

I must be the most clueless guy in the world. That never occurred to me. "If that's the case, she hides it pretty damn well."

Al took a deep breath and sighed. "And so do you."

In spite of her reaction at dinner, Delinda insisted on driving me out to the meetup point. I think I've made it clear that there's no arguing with her once she's made up her mind. Besides, the intersection of Sinatra and Royce was on the edge of town—too far to walk. Once we got there, I saw there was nothing for miles around except the roadways running through open desert and a few sun-battered "20 acres for sale" signs. I pointed out that there was no place for her to wait without being seen. She couldn't dispute that, and so reluctantly, she left me there. I wasn't sure, but I swore she looked worried. That expression was one I hadn't seen much on her, but I had to admit I liked it.

I glanced at my cheap wristwatch. It was one minute before eleven, and the nighttime temperature was hovering close to one hundred-five degrees. I was already beginning to sweat. Don't believe it when people tell you desert temperatures are bearable because it's "a dry heat." There's no such thing—and I had the wet armpits to prove it.

Suddenly, I heard a noise behind me and turned to see a beat-up Chevy sedan glide over next to where I was standing. The car was impossibly low to the ground, and at one time sported a garish purple metal-flake finish. However, the once bright and glittery paint was now dull and flat, courtesy of the desert sun. I also noted the fenders and doors were randomly dotted with rough patches of Bondo.

I could almost make out the silhouette of the driver through the dark, tinted windshield. There didn't seem to be anyone else in the car, so at least I wasn't going to be outnumbered. Still, it paid to be cautious; there was always the possibility that someone else was lurking in the back seat.

The passenger side window lowered, and an odoriferous cloud of marijuana smoke assailed me. The driver, a very large Latino male in a long black ponytail, leaned over. "Dude, get in," he said in a thick Hispanic accent. "We have a lot to talk about."

The guy was dressed in a soiled wife-beater T-shirt that revealed more skin art than bare flesh. The tattoos ringing his neck depicted a detailed collar of feathers that extended all the way up to his chin. A vividly realistic depiction of an owl's face overlaid his own features making him appear more avian than human. His eyes were so dark it was impossible to tell where his pupils ended and his irises began. Considering the amount of pot he was consuming that did not surprise me.

"Are you sure you're okay to drive?" I asked. It occurred to me that I might be in more danger letting the stoner haul me around in this heap than falling victim to a full-on ambush. "You look pretty blitzed."

The driver barked a laugh before he took a long pull from the thick joint that was burning in the ashtray. He exhaled slowly at the same time he replied. "Dude, you are as safe with me as in your madre's arms."

Obviously, the guy never met my mom. He held out the joint to me as I cautiously slid into the front seat. "No thanks, I'll pass."

He responded with a casual shrug. "Suit yourself, Dude."

No sooner had I closed the door than he took off. The Chevy sped up so quickly the acceleration pressed me back into the seat. Whatever he had under the hood, it was powerful and surprisingly quiet. I clutched the armrest hard and tried not to concentrate on the landscape flying by. By comparison, this guy made Delinda look like the safe driver of the year.

With some effort, I collected my wits enough to ask, "All right. Where are the girls? You said you knew where they are."

He laughed again. "Yeah, I did. But first, there are things you've got to know... About Section 14."

"What!" It was bad enough to be trapped inside a Bondo-mobile doing ninety miles an hour on a desert straightaway without having to deal with riddles. This was getting me nowhere, but it wasn't like I could just get out of the car. "I have no idea what you're talking about."

"Of course you don't. You're even ignorant about the magic in your face." He exhaled derisively, sending another cloud of smoke in my direction. "For a detective, you don't know shit. That's why you need to listen to what I'm going to tell you." He shot me a sideways glance and added, "Don't interrupt me again."

I shut up, mostly because I didn't want him to take his eyes off the road again. I reflected that this type of trap was one I could have never anticipated. As far as I was concerned, a more traditional ambush might be preferable compared to my present situation.

"This was all Iviatim land once, but the assholes in Washington didn't want to set any of it aside for its rightful owners. Instead, long before you were born, they decided that the railroad should come out this way. So, they divided all the land into one-mile-square parcels, like a giant checkerboard. They gave the odd-numbered parcels to the railroad company, and the even-numbered ones to the various bands of the Cahuilla tribe."

I cleared my throat, wondering what the hell all of this had to do with anything. "Okay, Okay! But what does all this have to do with the missing…"

He turned again to admonish me, looking more owl than human. "Shut up. I said don't interrupt. It's fucking rude." Thankfully, he returned his eyes to the road. "It was the land lease rules. Nobody wanted to develop the land the Indians owned when the government only allowed five-year leases… But in the sixties, when Palm Springs began to attract lots of money, the Feds changed the lease terms to ninety years."

"Then almost overnight, real estate became much more valuable, and now everyone wanted a piece… Especially the rich city people. The city officials decided that the tribal members were too stupid to administer their own land once the rules changed. A judge named Bolgert ruled that only caucasian agents could negotiate on the tribe's behalf in any land deals with developers. Then, when the money began to trade hands, Judge Bolgert and a bunch of his cronies took huge percentages of the deals they made. Some members of the tribe got real rich very quickly, but many others were left behind, trapped in poverty."

The name, Bolgert rang a bell, but I didn't dwell on it as the guy kept rambling on.

"Soon things got way worse. As the town of Palm Springs grew, land values went up even more. But, the folks that worked in the hospitality industries that were springing up couldn't afford to live in the developed portions of the city. They were forced to take up residence in the last parcel of Indian land that hadn't been sold off… Section 14."

"Hey," I finally said. "I appreciate the history lesson but…"

"Dude! What is it about don't interrupt do you not understand?" the driver snapped. He paused long enough to take another long drag off of the joint. "Close your yap and listen… The mayor of Palm Springs back then, William Hall, convinced a small group of the tribe's elders that the land was too valuable to let it be blighted by those lower class minority groups. Native Americans, Mexicans, Blacks, and so on."

Another name that rung a bell… Hall.

"First, they tried to freeze everyone out. Refused to hook up water lines, sewers or electricity. But the people held out. They dug their own septic systems, brought in their own water and managed to get along without any of the basic utilities enjoyed in every other part of town."

"Even though a select few in the tribe had profited greatly from many of the land deals, they realized that if they could reclaim Section 14 for development, there was even more money to be made. One of the tribe's elders, Fernando Lomas, secretly purchased much of Section 14 from members of his own tribe who desperately needed money. This man, Lomas, had a plan. With the help of the Mayor Bolgert, Judge Hall and a few others they decided to burn the whole square mile down. Every last bit of it. Folks went to work one morning only to return later that day to find their homes had been reduced to smoldering ruins. Some of those who were unlucky enough to be at home at the time, died in the fires, while the Palm Springs fire department sat by and watched. The very next day the bulldozers came and razed whatever was left. After that, the developers moved in, and more big money changed hands." Owl man shook his head in disgust. "Assholes!"

The bells were going off in my brain. Lomas, Bolgert, and Hall. Those were the last names of the missing girls. "Okay, you're implying the disappearances have something to do with what happened almost fifty years ago?"

"Some people will never forget," he replied.

"Why now? And where are the girls?"

The car screeched to a stop. Impossibly, we were at the intersection of Sinatra and Royce, exactly where we started. Owl man had a big smile on his face, and his black eyes glittered in the glow of the joint as he took another puff and blew the pungent cloud of smoke my way. "You're the detective, man. Figure it out."

I must have gotten a contact high because I don't remember getting out of the car. My only recollection was finding myself standing out in the street as the Chevy raced away and disappeared into the night. I was about to call Delinda on my cell when her Benz rounded the corner and drove up to where I was standing—in the middle of the road.

"Great timing," I said as I got into the car. "The guy just dropped me off."

"What do you mean?" she had an expression of genuine astonishment on her face that I had never seen before. "I only got a block away when I decided it wasn't a good idea to leave you alone, so I turned around and came straight back. You were right where I left you."

"That's not possible. I must have been gone at least for ten or fifteen minutes."

"Look at your watch, Tonnick."

I did. It was eleven O'clock straight up.

Delinda's expression grew darker. "Now, tell me everything that happened."

I ran it all by her. The stoned driver, the incredibly fast drive through the desert, the bit about Section 14 and the convergence of the missing girl's last names.

"I think we need to talk to Al," she finally said before she headed back to the hotel at a clip that rivaled my mystery driver.

Now it was my turn to be amazed. For once, Delinda Djinn had no answer.

Al was waiting for us when we got back to the hotel. He had staked out a secluded table in the cocktail lounge at the back of the room. After we joined him, I took the opportunity to order a well deserved straight shot of the most expensive tequila the bar served before I began to relate the entire experience, pausing only when the waiter arrived with my second round.

"The guy had a tattoo of an owl on his face?" Al asked. "You're sure?"

"Hell yeah," I replied. "His face was more ink than skin!"

Delinda glanced at Al expectantly. That in itself puzzled me. Usually, she was the one with all the answers, but now her uncertainty, and dare I say, her bewilderment, were all evident by her demeanor. That was also notable because as long as I've known her, she's always taken pride in her ability to revel in the unexplainable. Plainly, that was not the case now.

"So, what happened," Al prompted.

Delinda shook her head and addressed Al as though I wasn't in the room. "I drove off for only thirty-seconds before I decided it wasn't a good idea to leave him there by himself. I turned around and hurried back to find him standing in the road, right where I left him. He said he was gone for fifteen or twenty minutes, but by both of our watches less than a minute had passed." She paused for a moment as if she was reconsidering what she was going to say next. "I felt only the barest remnants of magic. Hardly a trace... But judging from what Mark said, it had to be powerful... Very powerful."

Great, I thought. Maybe it was the remnants of all the dope. "I'm sure there's a logical explanation," I offered—not that I had one at the moment.

Al acknowledged my protest with a nod. "That would be nice, wouldn't it?" He smiled and rubbed his chin thoughtfully before he spoke again. "But I don't think so. From what you've described, and what Delinda just said, it seems the Gods have smiled on you, Mark. Well, at least one of them."

"What the hell does that mean? Should I buy a Lotto ticket?"

He chuckled at my obvious confusion. "Your story reminds me of an old Native American legend that parallels your experience, without the Chevy of course. If I had to guess, I'd say you took a ride with Muut, one of the legendary Cahuilla spirit-gods."

I took a long pull on my drink. "What? The dope-smoking speedster was a what?"

"One of the ancient protectors of the Iviatim peoples," He spared me a wide grin. "Known to appear as an owl, among other things, guiding souls from this plane to the next."

"Al, did somebody slip a shot of bourbon into your ice tea? Really? Is that what you think?"

Al cocked his head and gave me a thin smile. "Maybe... Although what's truly hard to believe is why Muut appeared in that persona. Aside from selecting you."

"Very funny," I retorted.

"I wasn't trying to be funny. Usually, Muut's passengers end up in the afterlife. I can only guess at why Muut singled you out."

I thought about the clay embedded in my cheek as I turned to look at Delinda, hoping she'd offer another explanation. Right now, even delusional genie magic would make more sense than a reefer puffing god.

"Don't give me that look," she said. "Stopping time takes more..."

I didn't let her finish. "You were going to say, 'more magic than you have?'"

Without missing a beat, she shrugged.

I shook my head dismissively and quickly dismissed all of it as the kind of day-to-day malarky I've nearly grown used to. I've learned it's better not to argue. Instead, I asked, "If it was a powerful Native American spirit why didn't it cough up the location of the missing girls?"

"How do you know it didn't?" Delinda replied.

"Shit!" It suddenly hit me like a ton of bricks. "Can we find out which part of town used to be Section 14?"

"That's what the internet is for," Delinda replied, swiping away at her phone.

"What? No magic?" I teased.

"This is quicker," she shot back.

97

CHAPTER THIRTEEN

Section 14, California. Present Day.

THERE WAS NO WAY to be sure that the area formerly known as Section 14 would be where the missing girls—or their bodies—might turn up. But given the odd circumstances of how I came by the information, and the tenuous connections to the victims' families, I thought it was an excellent place to start. Besides, god or no, I didn't want to ignore the stoner in the Chevy. Regardless of what I believed, there were lives at stake and any lead, no matter how far-fetched, was worth looking in to.

Thanks to Delinda's research, I found that present-day Section 14 is a thriving part of downtown Palm Springs—a plethora of shops, hotels, and restaurants. Quite a far cry from the blighted neighborhood of the nineteen-sixties described by the guy with the owl tattoos. Ironically, that square mile also contained the site of the new Wiewa Tribal Cultural Center and Museum, which was now under construction. That location struck me as the logical place to start my search.

The morning following my encounter with the pot smoking tipster, Al and Delinda drove to the Palm Springs City Hall to research possible wireless providers who might be lobbying the city to displace AC&C's contract. On the way, I had them drop me off near the construction site. I did a quick walk around the area, and from what I could see, there appeared to be no one working there. Other than the sign and the excavation for the underground parking lot, construction seemed to have reached a standstill. Maybe they had run out of money, or were waiting for permits, but whatever the reason, the site was deserted.

I walked past the plywood fence with the poster announcing the future home of the museum and found the chain-link fence entrance to the site conveniently unlocked. Looking back, I should have known better. However, I continued on, observing the concrete forms and the rebar that was in place for what would become the underground parking garage. There was a sloping dirt ramp that led down, and I made my way to the bottom of the excavation for a better look. I was searching for anything that might be out of the ordinary, but so far, I found nothing of the sort.

I was about to climb up and out when I heard an engine startup nearby. A moment later a rain of concrete began to fall, knocking me off of my feet. I struggled against the crushing weight of the falling cement that was mercilessly pummeling me. Great gouts of the stuff were coming fast, and the loud engine and sloshing concrete were drowning out my yells for help. Frantically, I looked around for anything I could grab onto, but there was only a long vertical length of rebar about five feet away.

Swimming in liquid cement wasn't easy under the best of conditions, but the incessant rain of concrete made it even harder. I struggled through the heavy curtain of falling cement and over to the thin steel pole. The weight of my concrete soaked clothes made climbing up it a nearly impossible task. And worse, in the heat of the day, the cement was beginning to harden, cracking and flaking off of me as I fought to clamber up the skinny rebar pole, which was bending under my weight. I yelled again even though at this point I thought it was useless. Then, like a miracle, the flood of cement stopped, and I heard a voice from above.

"What the fuck are you doing down there?"

Usually, I have a wisecrack ready, but at this moment I was at a loss for words. Moments later, I saw the workman who had yelled come into view and then disappear. When he reappeared, he had a rope he threw down to me. Between him pulling, and me climbing, I eventually crawled free of the soupy cement. I looked at my rescuer.

He was a big potbellied guy, sweating profusely under his orange hardhat.

"Thanks, buddy," I said, wiping about five pounds of concrete off of my face.

"You could have been killed!" the man yelled angrily.

"No shit!" I agreed. "When I got here the place was deserted, why the hell were you pumping concrete?"

"It was my lunch break. Lucky for you I came back early when I saw the cement truck and the pumper. Normally, we don't pour this late in the day, but since I ain't the foreman who am I to argue?"

At that moment, another guy, much more fit than my rescuer ran up. "Tom, what the hell is going on? Who ordered the pumper? It's not scheduled…"

He stopped talking the moment he got a good look at me. I thought I looked dashing with a liberal coating of cement, but Delinda constantly reminds me I have no sense of fashion.

"What the hell! Who are you?" He said, turning to me. "How did you get here?"

"The fence was unlocked," I said gesturing with my arm, which cracked loudly as another piece of drying concrete flaked off and fell to the ground. "The place was deserted, so I thought I'd take a look around. That was when it started raining cement."

The guy shook his head. "Tom, you were supposed to lock up."

"I did, goddamn it," Tom protested. "I didn't know we were pumping today, but it's a good thing I got back here when I did… Otherwise, this guy would be buried under several tons of cement."

"Who the hell are you, and what are you doing here?" The guy asked, squinting at me suspiciously. He was obviously Tom's boss.

"My name's Mark Tonnick. I'm a private investigator." I reached for my creds in my back pocket. Fortunately, when I opened my wallet, the contents were relatively untouched. I held up my license trying to keep from smearing it with cement. "I'm looking into the disappearance of several missing girls. I got a tip to search in this area. Didn't realize I walked into a trap."

"What kind of tip?" the guy asked, suspiciously.

"A little bird told me," I replied, thinking there was more truth in that than I intended. "My source wishes to remain anonymous, but the tip was credible."

The boss's eyes widened. "I've heard about the girls. Hell, who hasn't. I'm Duane Commings, the foreman here. But you can see for yourself, there's nobody here."

"Yep. No girls. Only a lot of cement," I agreed.

"Yeah. About that… I need to have a conversation with those guys. They weren't supposed to be here now since the pour was scheduled for early tomorrow morning. They should all know better. This shit won't cure evenly when it's this hot." He shook his head in disgust and started out towards the street.

I followed Duane out the chain-link gate and watched as he walked over to a large cement truck. A chute on the rear of the rotating mixer was positioned over the trough of a large pumping apparatus attached to the back of a heavy-duty Ford pickup. The driver of the pickup was in an animated conversation with the cement truck driver which stopped as Duane and I approached. One look at me and it didn't take a genius to figure out what happened.

"What the hell are you guys doin' here?" yelled Duane. "I ordered the pour for tomorrow morning!"

"You called me a half hour ago," protested the cement truck driver. "Ordered me to get Cal and his pumper out here and start immediately."

"Bullshit! I never called you," Duane screamed in frustration. "Why would I order you to pump in the middle of the fuckin' day?"

Both men held their tongues as Duane continued ragging on them. "This is totally screwed up! You know all of this is going to crack! We'll have to re-pour at your expense!"

The fact that I was almost killed entered into no part of the conversation. While their blame-fest continued, I used my cement-crusted mobile to call Delinda to pick me up. I could hardly wait to see what she had to say. Fortunately, or unfortunately, depending on how you looked at it, I didn't have long to wait.

"What happened to you?" she said through the open passenger side window as she drove up alongside me.

"I decided to cool off with a little dip," I replied dryly.

"Really?"

"Actually, I walked right into a bit of an ambush." I went on to explain how I found the site deserted and ended up being pulled out of the unscheduled pour.

"See, somebody wants you dead!" she said with no small bit of satisfaction.

"It takes so little to make you happy," I said reaching for the door handle of the Benz.

"Oh, no you don't!" Delinda admonished. "Take off your pants!"

I did as she asked, even as folks walking by tried not to notice the guy who looked like a fugitive from a bad horror film peel out of his trousers. Good thing I wear boxer shorts. I folded up my pants, cracking off layers of cement before I got into the front seat.

"So, why is somebody trying to kill me?" I said, closing the car door. "It's not like I'm actually getting anywhere."

"There's got to be a reason," she said confidently. "I'm sure we'll find out what it is… Eventually."

"Great," I groaned. "I just hope it's before whoever wants me dead manages to succeed."

"Hopefully," she agreed.

There was no more conversation until we reached the hotel. I persuaded her to drive around to the rear entrance so I could sneak up to my room. I almost made it without being seen. On the trip up to my floor, I smiled at the elderly couple in the elevator with me. My friendly gesture resulted in more dried cement flaking off of my face. They didn't smile back.

After a long hot shower, I sat down at the desk in my room and started doodling on a notepad thoughtfully provided by the establishment. I made a list of what I knew at this point, which is not my usual process, but I was hoping that by resorting to pen and paper I could get something to click.

First, the discovery of the unconnected cable. Next, the missing girls —ostensively blamed on a dead Native American shaman awakened from the grave by said bogus cable. Then we, I mean I, get shot at, and Meena, who was in on the cable scam, is murdered in the course of the same afternoon. Then, later that same night, I get taken for a ride by a marijuana mystery man who promises to lead me to the missing girls, but instead gives me a history lesson about a section of town where I almost end up as part of the parking lot. Other than that, I had nothing concrete—pardon the pun. Even so, I was convinced my investigation was making someone nervous enough to kill me. I guess some might call that progress.

The phone on the desk rang, jarring me from my thoughts. I answered it on the second ring. "Tonnick, here."

"Mr. Tonnick, this is Miguel Knowle. We met at Mr. Ashton's estate."

"I remember. I suppose you've heard that the cable was a phony."

"Yes, I have, but few in the Wiewa tribe believe that."

"Then you need to spread the word that AC&C has nothing to do with whatever anyone thinks is happening here."

"Of course. However, getting people to listen, especially in light of Meena's murder won't be easy. Are you and your team available for a meeting this afternoon over at the Cultural Affairs Center to discuss this further? About three hours from now?"

"Sure," I replied. I wrote down the address and hung up. The brief conversation had only served to confirm what I already knew. Proving AC&C blameless was going to be murder.

CHAPTER FOURTEEN

Cahuilla Cultural Center. Present Day.

ON THE DRIVE OVER to our meeting with Knowle, Al brought us up to speed regarding his research at City Hall. According to him, the actual contract that AC&C held was only on a few cell towers placed on reservation land. The other part of the business was in carrier contracts which tribal members individually subscribed to at steep discounts. "No one in their right mind would spend a dime going after AC&C's contracts," Al said. "Truth is, I think the company loses money on their deal here."

"So, why would anybody want AC&C out?" Delinda asked. "From what you're saying, it wouldn't make sense." She turned a corner faster than I would have liked, sparing me a glance when I grimaced at the squeal of the tires on the blistering asphalt.

I was immediately sorry for my reaction as I knew it only encouraged her. "Maybe that's just a red herring," I offered without letting go of the door grip. "A convenient scapegoat to direct attention away from what's really going on."

"Okay," said Al. "Like what?"

I exhaled loudly. "Actually, I don't know... At least not yet." We took another turn on two wheels, but I resisted giving Delinda the satisfaction of seeing me squirm.

"Maybe we'll have a clearer picture after we talk to Knowle," said Delinda. "We're almost there."

Not soon enough for me.

Knowle was waiting for us when we arrived at the Wiewa Affairs Center. The building was an ugly, cement tilt-up in a nondescript industrial park just south of the city center. Immediately after we entered, the receptionist waved us in past stacks of crates and boxes.

"Dr. Schwartz will be joining us." Knowle glanced at his watch. "As a matter of fact, he should be here by now... Please excuse the mess," he added as we threaded our way around the rows of boxes and crates to join him. "We're in the process of moving everything into storage until our new building is finished."

"I've seen the new location," I replied. *From the bottom up.*

Knowle smiled broadly. "Good. Then you know it will be quite an upgrade... World class! In fact, some of our exhibits are already garnering attention in other parts of the country." He gestured towards several large wooden crates near the front door. "We're in the process of loaning our Section 14 exhibit to the Smithsonian Museum in Washington DC. We're expecting those to be picked up later today."

Section 14? I was going to ask him more about that, but Knowle had turned away to address the woman behind the reception desk. "Mercedes, would you mind giving Dr. Schwartz a call to make sure he's on his way?" He turned to us and added, "This is Mercedes. She's in charge of all our day to day... I don't know what we'd do without her."

We acknowledged his introduction with smiles and nods after which I got right to the point. "Mr. Knowle, perhaps you can tell us more about Section 14."

He frowned. "Sure, what would you like to know? It was an extremely dark time in our local history. We..."

"Miguel," interrupted Mercedes, "I left a message. He's not picking up." Her tone of voice conveyed more concern than I would have expected.

"That's odd," replied Knowle. "Howard always answers his phone... And he's usually never late, not where we're concerned."

Suddenly, the scar on my cheek started to itch. I've learned not to ignore that, which of course, is something I'd never admit to Delinda. "Does he live close by?" I asked.

"Yes," Knowle replied. "Only about five minutes away."

Delinda and Al both sensed what I was thinking at the same time. "Do you think we should head out that way?" she asked.

"Might be worth checking in on him," Al added. "He's had a rough time lately."

"We can take the van," Knowle said. "He once told me he had a drinking problem years ago. He showed me his AA chip. I'd hate to think he had a relapse over…"

He didn't need to complete his thought. I did it for him. "The way Meena was killed would challenge anyone's sobriety." I didn't mention that shortly before his phone call I was prepared to decimate the mini-bar in my hotel room for the same reason—it had been a rough morning. This meeting was the only reason for my change in plans.

The four of us piled into the Cultural Center's mini-van and drove off to Schwartz's place with Knowle at the wheel. As Knowle had said, Schwartz lived relatively close, and we arrived at his modest home in only a few minutes. After he pulled into the driveway, Knowle was the first one to reach the front steps. He rang the doorbell, but there was no response. Then, when he knocked on the door, it swung slowly inwards. Apparently, it had been left ajar. Again, I had a glimmer of the same feeling that struck me in Knowle's office. *The shit was about to hit the fan again.*

I wasn't all that surprised at what we found when we walked in and rounded the corner of the short entry hall. There, it the center of the living room, Dr. Howard Schwartz was lying spread-eagled in a pool of his own blood. There was a wide gash in his neck where his throat had been cut.

"Jesus Christ!" Knowle swore. "Is he…"

"Yeah, I'm sure he is," I interrupted.

Delinda kneeled down beside the corpse for a closer look at his wound. "The cut is jagged… Like from an animal's claw."

"Or a crude weapon," Al said pointing to the bloody stone knife that was lying several feet away under the glass-topped coffee table.

"Do you suppose he killed himself?" Knowle ventured. "Meena's death had to be a terrible shock."

"Hell no," I replied. "He definitely didn't commit suicide."

Knowle shot me a look that implied his amazement. "How do you know that?"

"Because the edge of the weapon is so dull it would have taken more strength than he could have applied by himself," I replied. "And, I doubt after ripping open his jugular he would have dropped the knife at his feet, not tossed it over there."

Knowle nodded and stood silent. The guy was plainly stunned at this turn of events.

"What I don't understand," Al said, "is why that particular weapon?"

I pointed to a display case at the far end of the living room which held a collection of stone implements. The cabinet's glass door was unlatched, and an empty space on one of the shelves indicated it was the likely source of the murder weapon. "Maybe it was a crime of opportunity. Perhaps his killer didn't come here with murderous intent but made that decision for some reason. Once they saw the knife in the cabinet, they made their move. It stands to reason that Schwartz knew his killer and didn't realize he was in danger until it was too late... Otherwise, there would have been more signs of a struggle. The attacker was brutal and quick. Poor guy probably never knew what hit him."

"Like Meena," said Al.

"Yeah," I agreed. "Like Meena."

Knowle finally snapped out of his daze. "I'm calling the police," he said punching 911 on his phone.

Great—it would be déjà vu all over again with the three of us discovering another body in less than forty-eight hours. It had to be a new record.

As I expected, it didn't take long for the Palm Springs homicide squad to show up. The lead detective was Wes Hembling, a portly man who had apparently little interest in pretending to be polite.

Particularly once he recognized our names from the case file he had inherited from the San Bernardino authorities. That was not surprising, considering San Bernardino County was on the brink of bankruptcy, Meena's murder case was the last thing they needed or wanted. Now, the Palm Springs PD found itself thrust into the middle of what would undoubtedly be two very expensive investigations.

Hembling grilled all four of us as long as he could, but he knew it wasn't going to get him anywhere. The man had his work cut out for him. His chances of lifting fingerprints off of the stone knife were about the same as finding them on the wooden handle of the war ax.

Thanks to Knowle being a well-known member of the Palm Springs community, our accounts had more credibility than they would have in different circumstances. However, that only went so far. Hembling's final words to us were the infamous, "Don't leave town without telling us."

Hembling's order to remain in town was unnecessary as far as I was concerned. We weren't done here—by a long shot. Other thoughts, besides the realization I've been stuck in desert climates far too often lately, were rolling around in my brain in no special order: The kidnapped girls. The planted cable. Meena—and now, Schwartz's murder. They were all undoubtedly connected, but how?

Once we all got back in the van, Al voiced the obvious question. "What would be the point of killing Schwartz?"

As soon as the words left his lips, the answer struck me. "I wonder if it was all about his credibility?"

"What?" Knowle said as he backed the van out of the driveway, deftly avoiding the patrol cars that were clustered in the street. "What are you talking about?"

I explained. "All of us... Including Schwartz saw the cable was a fake. The three of us can surely say it was planted there, but we're hardly an uninterested party... And without Schwartz to corroborate our findings, the entire tribal community is unlikely to believe it."

"Good point," Al said. "Somebody wants to keep the tribal members in fear of Tacquish's curse while still pointing the finger at AC&C."

From where I was sitting in the front seat, I saw Knowle's thoughtful expression. "Interesting… And insightful," he said. "Even with Howard's help, it would be an uphill battle to convince the community that the cable played no part in awaking the spirit of Tahquitz." He glanced at Al in the rearview mirror. "I noticed you refer to Tahquitz by his ancient Iviatim name. Not many people know that."

Al cracked a thin smile. "Force of habit, I suppose."

Man, you have no idea, I thought. However, there was something about Knowle's reply that struck me, even though I couldn't put my finger on it. "So, since we know the cable was a phony, Tahquitz couldn't possibly have come back. Right?" I asked.

Knowle didn't answer my question, but before I could press him further, he abruptly changed the subject as we pulled into the van's reserved space back at the Cultural Center's parking lot. "I'll request an emergency Tribal Council meeting tonight," Knowle said. "Everyone needs to know about what happened today." He turned off the ignition before he added, "I don't think it's a good idea for any of you to attend, given the circumstances. I'll call you later and let you know how it went."

He left us standing outside in the parking lot where it was of course, still hot as hell. I made towards the Benz in anticipation of the air-conditioned interior, but Delinda and Al didn't follow. I was out of earshot for a moment or two, so when I walked back to where they were, I asked them to repeat what they had been talking about.

"We were just discussing what could have brought back Tacquish," Al said.

"You can't be serious?" I protested.

"Yes, we are," Delinda flatly replied. "It wasn't the cable, but it could have been something else."

"What? Don't tell me you think someone brought him back on purpose?" *Holy shit! Did I just say that?*

"For once, you took the words right out of my mouth," Al quipped. "That's exactly what we were thinking."

I rolled my eyes. "I wasn't serious."

"Well, you hit the nail on the head, anyway," Delinda said without a trace of humor. "We'll wait for Knowle's call back at the hotel."

"Yeah," I agreed. "I wonder what the Tribal Council will think when they hear about Meena and Schwartz."

"You mean if they'll blame it on Tacquish," Al offered.

"And AC&C's cable to nowhere," I said sarcastically. "Too bad... Just when the stats on ghostly murders were starting to trend lower." I was prepared to deliver more pointed remarks along the same lines when my mobile rang. I recognized the voice immediately. It was Brent Todd, sounding soberer than the last time we spoke.

"What are you doing about my case?"

"I'm out of town, in Palm Springs..."

"Yeah, I know," he interrupted. "But I just found out something important."

"What's that?" I asked.

"Listen, you have to clear me... Now more than ever!"

"What are you talking about?"

"I'm going to be rich! But I need to be a free man to spend it."

Maybe he wasn't as sober as I thought. "What are you talking about?"

"I got a call today from a lawyer in New Jersey. He said my uncle died and left me a bunch of money in his will. I'm the only living relative."

"Okay. How much money?" I asked.

"About a hundred million dollars... Give or take."

My brain, trained by years of thinking the worst about people shot into high gear. "Did Lisa know about this?"

Todd hesitated before he replied. "No way, I just learned about it myself."

I cut him off. "Are you sure?"

"Of course I am! How would she find out?"

I sighed. He was plainly missing the big picture. No wonder he was only a mediocre cop. "I can only guess, but it would explain why she wanted you to sign that agreement."

Todd groaned as the very dim light bulb in his head turned on. "Shit! That bitch!"

I didn't reply. I wondered how Tommy the Shark got mixed up with Lisa in the first place. Random meeting? Or, could there possibly be a connection to the demise of Todd's late uncle?

"Hey... You still there, Tonnick?"

"Sorry, I was thinking," I replied lamely. The mundane aspects of his case were making me feel a whole lot better. After dealing with the possibility of resurrected evil spirits, a comparatively routine mystery about money was a welcome relief. "Tell me, what did your uncle do to amass such a fortune?"

Brent Todd cleared his throat. "Well, to be honest with you, I'm not sure. I never even met the guy. He was the black sheep in the family, or so I've been told. I remember hearing he might have been mixed up with organized crime in Jersey... But I don't know that for a fact."

Call me cynical, but now there were a hundred million reasons for me not to believe in coincidence. "I'm curious. When did your marital problems begin? Before or after the date of your uncle's death?"

"I'm not sure... The lawyer didn't tell me exactly when he died. Sometime last month, maybe."

"Do you know how? Was it natural causes?"

"I think the lawyer said he was killed in a car accident." There was a long pause. "Wait a minute... Do you think Lisa found out somehow?"

Fireworks began to explode in my brain. "Could be. I'll have to check."

"Well, don't take too long, Tonnick. I want to enjoy that money... You need to prove I'm innocent and keep me out of jail!"

I sighed. This news served to only complicate things further. His IA hearing was just a week and a half away, meaning I'd have to work fast once I got back to LA. "Don't worry, I've got a plan," I lied, not even bothering to cross my fingers.

"Shit. You better," Todd said as he clicked off.

Damn. When it rains, it pours.

"Are you working another case?" Delinda asked. "Don't you have enough on your plate already?"

"I owe this guy," I replied. "Delinda, you remember the article you quoted to me a while ago? About me losing my gun and what happened afterward?"

"What was that about?" Al asked.

"I was trailing a cheating husband. The guy jumped me and took my piece. Then he went home and killed his wife and kid before doing himself. It's why I'll never carry a gun again."

"Horrible," said Al. "But what's the connection?"

"The case I'm working on is for the late wife's brother. Like I said. I owe him."

CHAPTER FIFTEEN

Palm Springs, California. Present Day

AFTER WE HAD RETURNED to the hotel, the three of us made a beeline for what had become our de facto meeting place, the restaurant. When the waiter returned with my double Hendricks martini and Al's iced tea, we sent him away with our meal order. As always, Delinda had only requested a dinner salad. I was aware she was a vegetarian, but I realized during all the time I've known her, I'd never seen her eat very much. *Do genies actually need to eat?*

I dismissed those ridiculous thoughts and turned my attention to my drink. I was beat, and from the look of it, so was Al. However, as usual, Delinda looked as fresh as the metaphorical daisy. Even so, judging from the lack of conversation I surmised both of my table mates were as frustrated as I was. Nothing about this state of affairs was going particularly well.

I thought it was up to me to state the obvious. "So here we are at dinner again... The body count is rising, and the girls are still missing..."

Delinda nodded. "And, AC&C appears to still be on the hook for all of it."

"Seems so," agreed Al. "But what more can we possibly do?"

"We can Start by going through everything all over again," I replied. I had only taken a few sips, but my stomach was empty and the alcohol was already going to my head. Despite the effect of the gin, I still couldn't shake loose the thing that had been on my mind well before Schwartz's murder. "The whole Section 14 connection has been bothering me. I never got the chance to get more info from Knowle, and I can't shake the feeling we're missing something…"

"Wait," Delinda said smiling and arching a perfectly shaped eyebrow. "Are you saying you believe a tip you got from a supernatural source?"

"Come on," I objected. "I still don't believe there was anything supernatural about the guy… Anyway, I think the tip is good and we shouldn't ignore it." Both of them were smiling at me as I added, "I'm sure there's a rational explanation for the time discrepancy…"

Al shook his head. "I'm waiting to hear one, Mark."

"Ah, maybe Delinda was mistaken about the time… An' my watch is just a cheap Timex, anyway."

The food came, which was a good thing because my words were starting to mirror the influence of the gin, which was probably responsible for what happened shortly afterward.

Al excused himself from the table for a moment, and while he was in the washroom, I was liquored up enough to gather the courage-or the stupidity, depending on your point of view, to proposition Delinda.

"Ah, listen," I began, trying my best to sound casual. "After dinner, why don't you come by my room for a nightcap? We can go over things…"

She shook her head. "I doubt that's what you've really got in mind. Besides, you know I don't drink."

"Okay, so maybe my intentions aren't one-hundred percent honorable, but you have to know I…" The words got stuck somewhere between my brain and tongue, and there wasn't enough gin in the universe to set them free.

Surprisingly, she didn't laugh it off. Instead, she spared me a warm smile and a soft sigh. "Mark, I know how you feel about me. I really do. But it would never work out…"

"Why? We could try…" I interjected. I was going to add something juvenile—like "love conquers all," or something equally stupid, but she never gave me the chance.

She looked down at her hands before locking those gorgeous green eyes onto mine. "No, it would be a mistake. We can never be together... Not that way. Not ever."

I started to protest, but she reached over the table and took my hand in hers. "I understand you're slightly drunk, so I'm going to give you a pass... I will freely acknowledge there is a powerful bond between us, but we are from two different worlds... You will just have to accept that."

"I'm not sure that I can," I said softly.

"I hope I'm not interrupting anything, am I?" asked Al, as he reseated himself at the table.

"We were just discussing the case," I said, reluctantly releasing Delinda's hand and hiding my disappointment as best I could.

I expected him to come back with something snappy, but instead, he gave the two of us a thin smile. "I could see that... So, what about Section 14?"

Perhaps it was my wounded psyche deflecting after being let down by the object of my desire. Or, maybe it just clicked into my head all by itself. Regardless, there it was. "Knowle said there were a bunch of crates that were being shipped to the Smithsonian Museum."

"So?" asked Al. But I could see that Delinda understood where I was going with this.

"He said they contained the Cultural Center's Section 14 exhibits," I replied. "They might be long gone by now. He mentioned they were supposed to be picked up today."

"Not likely," she said, giving me one of her all-knowing smiles.

"Really? How come?" I asked, even though I knew she wasn't going to give me a straight answer.

"I think the shipper's truck broke down and he never got there."

Here we go again. "I suppose next you'll be telling me you made that happen."

"Only if you want me to," she replied demurely. "I had the same thought you did."

"Well, then," I nodded. "We need to get over there tonight and see what's in those crates."

"You mean, like, break-in?" Al made it sound like he was looking forward to it.

I gave Delinda a knowing smile. "I'm thinking that we'll probably find the door unlocked." She smiled back. *I wonder if she knows I'll never stop trying?*

We finished dinner quickly. I polished off my bone-in rib-eye and washed it down with two double espressos. The mega-caffeine dose had the desired effect—I wasn't bordering on tipsy anymore.

As we left the table, I glanced at my cheap Timex watch which had probably seen more time in Willy's pawn shop than on my wrist. It was ten past seven. We could be at the Wiewa Affairs Center in twenty minutes or less. With a little luck, Knowle would be off at the council meeting, and we'd have the opportunity to poke around before anyone was the wiser. What could go wrong?

CHAPTER SIXTEEN

Cahuilla Cultural Center. Present Day

WE KNEW WE WERE screwed the instant we drove into the parking lot. There were cars everywhere.

"I guess we know now where the Tribal Council is meeting tonight," Al said wryly. "What's the plan now?"

"I guess we play it by ear," I replied. "We'll just say we have a couple more questions we'd like to ask. What's the worst that could happen?"

Delinda shook her head. "Remember, Knowle said it wouldn't be a good idea if we showed up at the meeting."

"So, we'll say we forgot," I replied getting out of the car. I was going to add something else equally snarky when we heard sounds that had become all too familiar lately. Gunshots—lots of them, were coming from inside the building.

"Jesus! Haven't we been shot at enough?" Al exclaimed, joining me by the front entrance.

I pushed the glass doors open. "See, unlocked," I muttered as I rushed in to be greeted by the sounds of screaming and more gunfire.

One man, with a bloody forehead, ran past us punching in 911 on his mobile. "She's gone crazy!" he yelled as he fled into the parking lot and took cover behind a car. I could hear him telling the dispatcher a massacre was taking place at the Tribal Council meeting.

"I think our timing stinks," I said.

"You think?" Delinda had come up behind Al and me.

The three of us had hunched down behind a row of wooden crates nearest the entryway. The gunfire continued, sounding like it was coming from deep inside in the building. Suddenly, the sounds stopped, leaving an eerie silence in their wake. Even so, we waited until we thought it was safe to continue further on into the building. Not knowing what to expect, we kept close together, ready to seek cover behind the random stacks of crates and boxes that filled the reception area.

When we reached the first hallway, I squatted low to the ground and chanced a quick glance around the corner. The corridor was empty, and a door labeled, "Conference Room 1" was swung wide open. I motioned for Al and Delinda to stay back and crept forward until I could peer inside the room—being careful to remain as low as possible behind the doorframe.

Inside, the scene was as bloody as it was surreal. Eight men and four women were slumped over the table, all apparently shot as they sat in their seats. I saw that Knowle wasn't among them, nor was there any sign of the shooter. Sounds of soft groaning reached my ears, and I realized that one of the men lying face down on the table was still alive. I crept into the room, keeping my head down until I thought it safe to stand.

Once I reached the wounded man's side, I gently pulled him back off the conference table and into his chair. The bullet had penetrated his left shoulder, which was bleeding profusely. I tore off a piece of his white dress shirt and stuffed into the wound to staunch the flow of blood. That was all I could do for now, I hoped it would keep him alive until help could arrive.

Al and Delinda had joined me and were checking others around the table. Apparently, the man I had triaged was the only one alive. "Be careful," I warned. "I haven't seen the shooter, but they still might be close by."

Ironically, those words of warning were followed by a loud flurry of weapon fire. Usually, I don't mind being right, but this wasn't one of those times. I dove for the floor at the same time as Mercedes, the receptionist we had met earlier that afternoon, barged into the conference room, firing madly in all directions. I didn't get a good look at her face, but I got the impression she was grinning from ear to ear.

At that moment, I thought we were all goners. Propelled by my instinct for self-preservation, I crawled under the heavy wood conference table. That was when the scar on my face to started itching —my crazy friends would have me believe that signified magic was at work. Seconds later, a large portion of the suspended ceiling overhead inexplicably collapsed directly on top of the hapless shooter.

Surprised and distracted, Mercedes stopped firing as the rain of acoustic panels, wire and T-rails crashed down. She hesitated long enough for Al to bring her down in a flying tackle worthy of an Oakland Raider. As they both slammed onto the floor, the automatic pistol skittered out of her hand and across the room. Still on my hands and knees, I scrambled like a crab fleeing a pot of boiling water until I reached the Smith and Wesson. As soon as it was in my hands, I pulled out the clip and ejected the cartridge remaining in the breech.

When I got back onto my feet, I saw that Delinda was still standing where I had seen her last. Evidently, she had felt no need to escape the gunfire by taking cover under the table. Immediately after the ceiling came down, my scar had stopped itching. Coincidence? Or was I just discounting the obvious? The owl man had mentioned something about me ignoring the magic in my face. But, at this point in my life, I'm just fine with that.

Mercedes kept on fighting furiously, trying to escape Al's grasp, but he had wrapped both arms around her, pinning her tightly. Then, with one loud and incoherent scream, she made the poor choice of trying to bite Al's wrist. Unfortunately for her, she chomped down on his plastic and metal prosthesis, which was clearly not what she expected.

Roaring in frustration, she spat out a bloody broken tooth and began muttering gibberish in a voice that sounded less human and more like the hissing of a snake. I hurried over to help Al, but there was no need. By the time I reached the other end of the room, her struggling abruptly stopped, and she had wilted into Al's arms like a deflated balloon.

"Whoa! What the hell got into her?" I said.

Al looked down at the woman hanging limply in his grasp. "Not what... Who."

I put two fingers on her carotid artery. There was no pulse. "We won't have a chance to ask her. She's gone."

The sounds of approaching sirens were growing louder. The paramedics and cops would be here in seconds. "What do you suppose they'll make of us being here?" I asked.

It was a rhetorical question. Predictably, Hembling and the team of homicide detectives we saw earlier in the day were not happy to see us again. Nor, were they initially willing to dismiss our presence as an unfortunate coincidence. Luckily, the man who had sped past us dialing 911 as we entered, corroborated our arrival on the scene while the shooting was in progress. He even went so far as to credit us for saving his life.

Hembling appeared disappointed he had no good reason to arrest us since there was no law against being in the wrong place at the wrong time. However, we hadn't accomplished what we came here to do in the first place, and now matters were complicated further by our stumbling into an incomprehensible and gigantic mess. Despite the present circumstances, I was determined to follow through with our original intention of inspecting the crates.

My main takeaway from boot camp had always been that it was "better to ask for forgiveness than to beg for permission." So, while the bodies were being taken out on gurneys, I took the opportunity to make my way over to one of the three crates addressed to the Smithsonian Museum.

Before anyone could figure out what I was doing, I grabbed a Native American milling stone off of Mercedes's nearby desk. She had used it as a paperweight, but I employed it as a hammer, banging away at the wooden edges of one of the crates until it loosened enough for me to grab ahold of it and pry off the side.

The sound of my rock hammer and splintering wood brought several cops running, but by the time they reached me I had found what I was looking for. Tied up tightly inside the crate was a girl I recognized from her photo in the brief. It was Janis Lomas. She seemed more dead than alive, but the officer who rushed up intending to cuff me ended up lending me a hand in pulling her out of the crate. The cop wisely screamed for a paramedic as we were untying her. I put two fingers on her neck and felt a faint pulse, a fact that was confirmed by the responding paramedic. She was alive, but only barely.

Several other first responders assisted me in taking apart the other two crates that were bound for DC. Inside those, we discovered the other two victims, Marie Bolgert and Kelsey Hall. They were in the same condition as Janis—drugged, dehydrated, and on the brink of death.

I stood back, giving the medical personnel room to do their thing. "Good thing those crates weren't picked up today," said Delinda, who was now standing behind me.

"Yeah, lucky break," I replied turning to face her. "Or whatever…"

She returned my smile. "Or whatever."

We watched the paramedics hook up IV's while they rolled the girls out to the ambulances. I knew that after they recovered, the authorities would question them in hopes of finding out what happened. After everything that had gone on, I felt it was doubtful that anyone would ever learn the truth.

"How did you know they'd be in there?" bellowed detective Hembling as he rushed up to where the three of us were standing. He looked at me as though I had put them there myself.

"Just a hunch," I said. "All the girls came from families that had greatly profited from the Section 14 tragedy. We came here to check out the connection and found all hell breaking loose."

Hembling didn't try to disguise his exasperation. His demeanor was one I'm all too familiar with—especially from cops. "Why didn't you say anything about this earlier this afternoon?"

"Because detective, I didn't put it all together until afterward. Besides, it could have been nothing…"

He exhaled loudly and waved me off. "A good thing it wasn't. Another couple of hours and the girls wouldn't have made it. They tell me it's gonna be touch and go for them as it is."

"But, we didn't get here soon enough to save those folks," Al said, motioning to several body bags being brought out on gurneys.

"Yeah. Nothing you could do," Hembling offered. "That crazy woman wiped out almost the entire Tribal Council."

"One is missing," I said. "Knowle."

"Was he here?" the detective asked.

"He was supposed to be," Delinda said. "He told us he was going to call the council meeting when we left him earlier today."

Hembling stroked his double chin. "We'll find him... One way or another. All of you, stay out of this. It's police business and none of yours. Do I make myself clear?"

"Yes, sir," Delinda replied sincerely. Of course, nobody reminded Hembling that he specifically requested we not leave town.

"Then, get the hell out of here."

We quickly complied with his request and got back into the car. The outside nighttime temperature at 8:30 was still one hundred plus, and the interior of the Benz felt like an E-Z bake oven. With the engine running and the air conditioner blasting, we watched as the last of the ambulances left the lot. Only the police cruisers and forensic team's van remained.

I didn't wait for Delinda to throw the car into gear before I put the question to Al. "What did you mean in there when you said, 'not what, who?'"

"You're not going to like it, Mark. I can tell you that," Al replied. "That gal, Mercedes, was possessed... By Tacquish's spirit."

"Are you sure?" Delinda asked before I could register the very emphatic protest I was preparing to deliver.

"Positive. Right before she chomped on my fake hand, she said something in the old Ivia language... In a voice I'll never forget. It was him... No doubt in my mind."

"Fabulous theory," I snapped. "Medicine man comes back from the dead, possesses the receptionist and kills the Tribal Council? And what about the kidnapped girls? Did the dead guy do that too?" I made no attempt to hide my sarcasm. "And where the hell is Knowle?"

"Told ya, you wouldn't like it," Al said without even the faintest trace of a smile.

"I'm sorry you don't see the humor in all of this!" I retorted.

"The only thing I find funny is that you can't ever believe what's right in front of your nose," he replied.

"What I find hard to believe is that everything happening in my life lately comes down to magic, evil spirits... And reefer puffing owl gods!"

"Well, regardless of what you think, the tip panned out and the girls are safe," Delinda interjected. "And, we proved the cable was a fake. Both big wins."

"Okay, I agree," I sighed. "But that brings me back to the elephant in the room. If Al's right... And I'm not saying he is, but the for the sake of argument, if the cable didn't bring back Tahquitz, what did?"

"Or who?" Delinda added. "And why?"

"I can't even believe we're having this conversation," I mumbled.

"It's about time you did," Delinda replied. "Because if we answer that question, we can put an end to all of this."

"Well, that's clearly out of the range of my expertise," I said.

"But not mine." Delinda gave me a cryptic look before she tore out of the parking lot.

Here we go again. Down the rabbit hole... At breakneck speed.

CHAPTER SEVENTEEN

Bing Crosby Estates, California. Present day

WE DIDN'T HEAD BACK to the hotel. Instead, Delinda announced we were going to Knowle's address.

"Don't you think the cops will have the same idea?" I said.

"They might. But, I don't think they have the proper information on file," Delinda replied.

"Oh, and you know this how?" I asked.

"The same way I knew the crates were never picked up," she said slyly. "The police will be delayed long enough for us to take a look around before they get there."

Typical genie stuff. "So... If he's not at home, will we find the door unlocked?" At this point, I found it hard not to be snarky.

Delinda's reply was no less condescending. "Why don't we wait and see?"

We turned the corner past a sign that read "Bing Crosby Estates," and pulled into the second driveway of the quiet residential neighborhood. The house was dark, except for a faint glimmer of light seeping through the closed drapes of the front window.

"Looks like nobody's home to me," Al ventured.

"One way to find out," I said stepping out into the stifling nighttime heat. I knocked twice and rang the doorbell before I tried the door handle. It was locked. Delinda and Al had joined me on the front steps.

"No luck?" Al commented.

I shook my head. "No, it's absolutely..." I was going to say, "locked" when Delinda strode up and effortlessly opened the door.

"You were going to say?" she remarked dryly.

I resisted my impulse to take the bait. Instead, I gently pressed ahead of her to make sure I was first through the door. "Age before beauty," I said hoping I wouldn't end up stopping a bullet.

"In that case, I..." Delinda didn't finish her sentence.

There was no body spread out on the floor, but the scene in the living room was bizarre enough to stop all of us in our tracks. The light in the adjoining kitchen had been left on, illuminating the strange tableau before us. The furniture was pushed back against the walls, and the carpet had been split and rolled back exposing the bare concrete foundation in the center of the room. However strange that was, it was the dead owl in the center of the intricate drawings on the floor that sent goosebumps of dread racing up and down my neck.

"This is bad, very bad," pronounced Al.

"No kidding," I replied. "What the hell happened here?"

Al kneeled down to examine the bloody bird. "Now we know how Tacquish has returned. I've thought this ritual was only a rumor. Even way back then, it was only whispered in fear. That someone would attempt to recreate it is unthinkable."

In spite of myself, I said, "Are you saying that Knowle has brought him back?"

Al nodded grimly. "That's what it looks like. The drawings and the sacrifice of the owl are symbolic of the god Muut, an act that is beyond sacrilegious. In the days of the Lake Tribes, it would have warranted death to even contemplate such a ceremony."

I was reluctant to ask, but I did anyway. "So, do you really believe that a dead owl and some scribbles on the ground can bring back the dead?"

Al glanced up at me and then at Delinda. "Yes, I do. Without a doubt, Knowle has freed Tacquish's spirit."

From his expression, I guessed that wasn't the worst of it. "And..." I prompted.

Al stood and looked warily around the room before he replied. "And, if the old legends are true, Tacquish's spirit can pass from host to host... Body to body."

I sensed where he was going with this, and I hated myself for coming to the obvious conclusion. "You mean like Tahquitz went from Knowle to Mercedes? She was possessed? You realize how crazy that sounds?"

Al didn't answer, but Delinda did. "What anyone thinks doesn't really matter. This isn't over yet, is it, Al?"

"I'm afraid not," Al replied shaking his head. "Knowle is the nexus for Tacquish's spirit. He might even be controlling its power, at least for now."

"So, even if that's possible, why did Knowle want to murder the Tribal Council?"

"I don't know. Perhaps it was Tacquish, seeking vengeance. Knowle could be losing control of the spirit... Or perhaps, he never had control."

I couldn't resist. "So then why did Mercedes use a gun? Why didn't the evil spirit just eat their souls or something?"

Al shook his head as if I had asked a serious question. "Legends say, when a spirit possesses a living being, it doesn't have any magical powers."

"I guess that's good news," I quipped. "If it's true."

Al hadn't caught my sarcasm. "We'd better hope so. If Tacquish's spirit were to materialize and assume his own physical form, he would be unstoppable." Al looked at Delinda and added, "By anyone or anything."

"So now what?" I asked.

"We should leave," Delinda said. "The police will be here soon. We surely don't want to explain our presence to Detective Hembling... Again."

We wasted no time in piling back into the Benz. Delinda drove away from the house in the opposite direction from where we had come. Headlights appeared turning around the corner behind us and pulling into the driveway of Knowle's place. Without a doubt, it was Hembling and his crew.

I breathed a sigh of relief. "Good timing for a change. Any suggestions as to where to begin looking for Knowle?"

"Unless I'm mistaken," Al said. "He'll be looking for us."

We decided to return to the hotel. There was no point in searching for Knowle—once Hembling saw what we found in Knowle's living room, he'd be on that in a New York minute. After we arrived at the hotel, the three of us took the elevator up to the 3rd floor where our rooms were. We were in the midst of a conversation about whether to return to LA or not. However, by the time we had reached the door of my hotel room, the discussion had turned into an argument.

"I'm not inclined to leave either," I said, replying to Al's insistence that we stay until Knowle was found. "But maybe it's best to let the cops sort it out," I argued reaching for my key card. "We accomplished everything we were sent here to do and more, now…"

The door opened suddenly before I could even wave my card over the lock. "Well, well. Look who it is… Mr. Tonnick and his friends," said the shorter of the two thugs. He was aiming his snub nose .38 at my chest with a self-satisfied grin. I recognized both of them as the guys who had visited my office looking to rearrange my face.

The tall guy was standing next to him, smiling broadly. "Thought you'd seen the last of us?"

"I had hoped so," I said half under my breath, confident he wasn't going to shoot me in the hallway.

"Okay wise ass. We'd do you right here, except somebody would like to talk to you," Shorty replied.

"What about these two?" asked the tall man.

Shorty punctuated his answer with an ominous bark of laughter. "Bring 'em along. They seen our faces."

I looked at Al and Delinda. They appeared confused at this turn of events that were plainly unrelated to phony cables, resurrected shamans or murderous receptionists.

"Let's go," urged the tall thug. "And don't try anything or your friends'll take a slug in the back."

"I'm assuming we're going to have a chat with Tommy the Shark?" I said while we headed for the stairs. Al and Delinda both gave me questioning looks.

"Shut up. You'll find out soon enough," spat the short guy.

I had to give them credit. Tall and Short had scoped out the hotel thoroughly enough to get us outside through the back door and into the parking lot without being seen by any of the hotel's guests or staff. They ordered the three of us into an impressively restored 60s Lincoln Continental. It was one of the limited editions, with suicide doors and dark tinted windows. At least we were being abducted in style. I sat in the middle of the leather backseat, flanked by Al and Delinda as the tall guy got behind the wheel. Shorty sat in the front passenger seat, facing us with his Saturday night special pointed at me.

"Who the hell are these guys?" Al whispered.

"Shut up!" Shorty snapped.

None of us saw any point to further conversation, so we sat quietly while the Lincoln made its way through the city center and onto an unlighted straight away through the desert. About fifteen minutes later we passed a sign that welcomed us to Desert Hot Springs. Several turns later, the car pulled into the driveway alongside a late model Porsche. The ritzy, mid-century modern, ranch-style house sat on an isolated lot by itself, making it an ideal location for a mob boss's vacation getaway. In light of Tommy Rosselli's reputation, I didn't think we'd be riding back to our hotel any time soon. For once, I hoped Delinda might use one of her genie magic tricks to get us out of this mess. I could always deny it later.

"Out," snarled the short thug as he came around to open one of the backseat doors. "Don't try anything funny!" The tall guy opened the other. He had much better taste in artillery, evidenced by the automatic he was holding.

We were ushered into the house and onto the back patio. I was somewhat relieved to see there was no plastic sheeting spread out over the flagstone. I took that as a good sign. What was not so good, was that Tommy Rosselli was there, sitting comfortably in a white wicker chair puffing on a cigar. His expression changed from bad to worse as his crew marched us in. "Louie! Who the fuck are all these people?"

The short guy shook his head and shrugged. "Sorry, Tommy. They were with Tonnick when we snatched him."

"Yeah," agreed the tall thug. "What were we supposed to do?"

"Dummies! Can't you get nothin' right?" snapped Rosselli. He ran a manicured hand through his thinning hair and took another drag on his cigar as his "associates" looked meekly on. He got out of his chair and walked over to Al and got in his face. "Okay Tonnick, we're going to have a little…"

Louie cleared his throat and motioned to me. "Uh Tommy, this is…"

Evidently, Rosselli wasn't fond of looking like an idiot. He dismissed Louie with an angry wave and put his face next to mine. "Listen, Asshole, you're going to tell me everything, or I start by hurting your friends…" He turned to Delinda and gave her a lecherous leer. "Starting with the lovely lady here. Fingernails are my favorite…"

His threat was interrupted by several loud hoots from a nightbird just outside the patio.

"What kinda fuckin' bird is that?" Rosselli snarled.

"I think it's an owl, boss," replied the tall guy.

The bird's cries began again. This time they were even louder.

"Frank, go outside and put a bullet in the goddamn thing an' shut it up!"

Frank made to leave, but the sound stopped as suddenly as it began. "I think it heard you, Tommy," he joked.

"I hate the fuckin' desert," Rosselli remarked.

"Me too," I said.

"Who asked you, wiseguy?" he poked a fat finger into my chest to make his point.

"Nobody," I shrugged. "But you don't need to hurt anyone… I'll tell you what you want to know." I figured if I stalled for time, an opportunity to escape might present itself. I shot a quick glance at Delinda who appeared unconcerned. That was almost encouraging.

"Don't try to bullshit me," Rosselli threatened. "We bugged Todd's phone. How do ya suppose we knew you came down to the Springs? My guys also saw you takin' pictures at the Grill in LA, so don't take us for idiots!"

That was puzzling. If he knew so much, what did he need to ask me about? I figured I'd find out soon enough—probably right before they killed us. "So, then you know he hired me to investigate the faked evidence regarding his supposed theft of fifty grand from the LAPD property room."

"Don't fuck with me. What I want to know is if you told Todd or anybody else about me."

"Nope. Never got the chance to tell Todd. Not even my friends here. You obviously overheard the details I've shared with Todd on the phone."

"How do I know you're telling the truth?" Rosselli growled.

"Come on, what more do you need? Besides, even Todd will be able to put it together... Eventually."

Rosselli laughed derisively. "I doubt that. How that shit ever became a detective is beyond me."

I resisted the temptation to agree with him. Instead, I said, "When he manages to connect the dots he'll figure you were involved." Rosselli gave me a look that suggested I keep talking, so I happily obliged him. "I have to say though, I haven't had time to check to see if you and Todd's late uncle were connected somehow." Rosselli tried to keep his expression neutral, but he wasn't doing a very good job of it. I decided this was why he was grilling me—and who am I to disappoint, so I hit him with my best guess. "If that were the case, it might not be much of a stretch to assume you even had the guy killed. Auto accidents can be staged." I paused waiting for a reaction.

"Go on," Rosselli prompted. His thin smile was an informative tell.

"Then, you found out about the will... And the dollar amount attached to it. When you discovered he left everything to his only next of kin, Brent Todd, that was when you put your plan into action. You figured the cleanest way for you to get your hands on the money was through Todd's wife, Lisa. Pretty bold, but with her husband in prison, she would control the inheritance... Along with you of course."

Rosselli sneered, unable to contain himself any longer. "It was my fuckin' dough in the first place! Mine! For the last ten years that guy in Jersey was laundering money for me. When I found out he was skimming off the top, I had him whacked. It was only afterward that I found out he also laundered the cash he stole from me. An' if that ain't enough, I come to find he left it to his only surviving relative. A fucking cop! Probably just to spite me!"

Todd's uncle was a smart man, I thought. He was probably aware that if he turned up dead, it wouldn't be due to natural causes. Petty revenge is better than none at all. "So, am I to assume that you framed Todd, so he'd go to prison leaving Lisa, and presumably you, to get the fifty-million? I also think you'd make sure that Todd didn't last very long once he got there."

I noticed that Rosselli's features were hardening as I spoke. Maybe he didn't like appearing so transparent, not that I cared, so I went on. "I'll bet marriage is also in the picture for you two lovebirds."

"Not bad, for a fuckin' private dick... Or just a dick." He laughed at his own joke, but that was cut short by an earsplitting burst of owl sounds again.

From the look on Rosselli's face, I could tell the noise was getting on his nerves. In truth, it sounded like the bird was inside the patio. I saw Delinda was smiling at Rosselli's discomfort, though he was too distracted to notice. When I managed a brief questioning glance in her direction, she responded with a quick wink.

Her reaction gave me more hope than I felt at that moment. And, it decided me that our best bet was to continue playing for time. The one sure way to do that was to give Rosselli an opportunity to stroke his own ego. "You must have made a pretty big play to get Lisa to help you."

Rosselli chuckled. "Not really. Her husband is so self-involved that she was hungry for someone to come along who would pay attention to her... And I've always been great with women. She practically flew into my arms."

Works every time. Thinking there was no reason not to press my luck, I joked, "You realize, relationships formed after a breakup don't last very long."

"So true," Rosselli agreed with a smarmy grin. "Lisa's shitty in bed so our marriage won't be sweet, but it will be short." He took another pull on his cigar and looked straight at me. There was no humor in his expression this time. "So, you didn't mention my name to Todd on the phone, that much is for sure... And we both know he won't be able to put it any of it together on his own... At least not until it's too late."

"Well, he knows he's been framed," I replied, still hoping I could give Delinda time to throw a fireball or something. "But, I have to give it to you, you did a good job with the evidence... He's totally screwed."

"Ain't that too bad," Rosselli leered. "Yeah. I thought of everything. The payoff to the evidence clerk was easy... Guy has a Jones for gambling... And I have some pull with a few folks in Vegas that were looking to break his arms if he didn't pay up. I bought up his markers and made him a deal he couldn't refuse."

"Smart," I nodded. "And you faked the video?"

"Easy peasy. Lisa sent me a picture of Todd's ring... An' did you know you can find just about anything on eBay? I bet I paid less for his class ring than he did!"

"So, to seal the deal you had to put the stolen cash into Todd's account. That must have hurt," I offered.

"Not really. That was the icing on the cake. Fifty-grand for fifty-million. A real no brainer." He flicked ash off his cigar onto the flagstone. "Well, Tonnick. I think we're done here. I'm headed back to LA, and you have an appointment with destiny." He looked at Al and Delinda. "And, I suppose I can't count on your friends to keep a secret either."

"Hey," interjected Al, "what are you planning to do with us?"

"I thought that was obvious," Rosselli replied. "Louie and Frank are going to take the three of you out for a little ride through the desert."

He nodded towards his two thugs, and they proceeded to zip tie our hands behind our backs. I looked over at Delinda expectantly, but there were no magical fireworks or any other helpful supernatural events. She smiled broadly as the owl started up again, screeching louder than ever.

"I can't take this shit anymore!" Rosselli yelled. He left the patio with his hands over his ears. "Call me when it's done!"

CHAPTER EIGHTEEN

Desert Hot Srping, Present Day

AT GUNPOINT, FRANK AND Louie marched us back to the driveway where we resumed our places in the rear seat of the Lincoln. As the car pulled onto the roadway, I whispered to Delinda. "What are you waiting for?"

"I don't have the faintest idea of what you're talking about," she replied coyly.

"You know," I protested.

"I thought you didn't believe in magic."

"Shut up," growled Louie. Evidently, the short guy wasn't prone to speaking in complete sentences.

"Who cares," argued Frank who was piloting the car towards the open desert. "They'll be quiet soon enough."

"Come on, Delinda," Al said in a voice so low I had difficulty hearing it, "What's the plan?"

"You'll see," she said.

"I can't wait," I murmured.

"Shut up, or I'll do you right here!" Louie barked.

"No, you won't," I countered. "You'll screw up this fine vintage automobile. You're not going to put a bullet hole in a 60s Lincoln." I guess he agreed with my assessment because the last thing I remembered was him slamming his gun onto the top of my head. I guess a little blood on the car seat was no big deal.

When I came to, the car had stopped, and I found myself roughly hauled out of the back seat to join Delinda and Al standing by the Lincoln's open trunk. I was groggy, but aware enough to know we were standing in the desert. It hurt to turn my head, but there was nothing to see except empty landscape for miles.

"Louie, grab the shovels," Frank directed.

The short thug took two shovels out of the trunk as Frank waved his gun at us. "Start walking."

I wanted to rub my aching head, but my hands were still zip tied behind me. The nighttime air was so hot I could feel the drying blood from my split scalp beginning to itch.

"Are you okay?" Delinda said. It was nice to hear the worry in her voice.

"Never better," I replied.

"I can tell from his sarcasm there's no brain damage," Al said dryly.

"Shut up and keep walking," Louie snapped.

Since none of us were in a position to argue, we trudged on silently for another ten minutes until Frank announced, "That's enough."

Louie threw the shovels he was carrying on the ground and cut the zip ties off of Al and I. "Pick up the shovels and dig," he ordered, waving his gun.

"Why? You're just going to shoot us anyway," I argued.

"You are so right," Louie smirked and fired his gun point blank at my head. I didn't hear the gunshot, only the screeching of an owl. Instinctively, I shut my eyes. There wasn't enough time to formulate any last thoughts until about a second later when I realized I was still alive.

I freed my eyes, but I couldn't believe what I saw. Louie stood frozen in place, the bullet from his gun suspended in mid-air, halfway between the barrel and my head.

"Dude, can I give you and your friends a lift?"

I twisted my head and for the second time in so many seconds, doubted what I was seeing. The lowered Chevy with the owl-faced stoner was idling only yards away from where I was standing. The front passenger side door was open, and I saw Al and Delinda were already sitting on the back seat. Their eyes were closed, and they both appeared to be asleep. *What the hell?*

I was shaken but still had enough sense not to look a gift god in the mouth. I climbed into the front seat and closed the door.

"Are you sure you don't want a hit," the owl god offered while blowing a pungent cloud of smoke my way. "You might find it... Enlightening." He held out the thick joint.

Don't ask me why I took it—I haven't smoked dope since high school, but I felt compelled to accept his offer. As I took a shallow puff, he put the Chevy in gear, and we roared away. I thought I heard a distant gunshot a moment later. I had no sooner handed the joint back when everything around me dissolved away. It was a sensation I had only experienced after standing up too quickly from a hot bath. The word, "psychedelic" didn't do justice to it.

When my vision cleared, I was standing in Knowle's living room. It was as if I were an unseen bystander in someone else's dream. Knowle was nearly naked, save for the sash of leather slung low across his thighs, and his face was anointed in broad streaks of black paint or ash. I watched as he wrung the neck of the owl so viciously its head was partially severed from its neck. The wretched creature was still twitching in his hands as he dripped its blood over the chalk drawings on the concrete floor. All the while, he was chanting in a strange, unworldly melody. The words were sibilant and harsh, sounding as if they were never meant to be uttered by a human tongue. Somehow, I knew I was witnessing events through a window into the past— watching Knowle when he had summoned Tahquitz's spirit from the dead.

The owl's blood sizzled as it dripped onto the sigils as if it had struck a hot pan. Knowle threw the carcass onto the boiling puddle of blood, falling silent as a thin, dark, vaporous mist rose from the mangled body of the dead bird. The mist grew thicker and more defined until it coalesced into the semi-transparent outline of a man. The long-dead shaman was being resurrected in front of my eyes as I stood, unable to move or speak. Suddenly, the man's form melted into vapor again and encapsulated Knowle from head to toe.

As the spirit cloud gradually disappeared into Knowle's physical body, his eyes rolled up impossibly far into his head, leaving only a white blank stare. When he shut his eyes and opened them again, there were huge red holes where his pupils should have been. Then, he began walking towards me as if he knew I was there, looking on.

Thankfully, the scene dissolved away once more. Again, I found myself still an incorporeal observer, hovering unseen outside the conference room at the Wiewa Cultural Affairs building. Knowle was standing there, now dressed in a three-piece suit and tie, as Mercedes approached him with an armful of papers. Somehow, I knew she was about to tell him that the truck they were expecting to pick up the shipping crates had broken down. But, she never got the chance. Before she could speak, the vaporous outline of Tahquitz left Knowle's body and engulfed her in a sentient mist. Gasping for breath, Mercedes dropped the papers she was holding. Then, her expression of horror melted into something far more sinister. Now she was smiling maniacally as she wordlessly accepted the gun Knowle handed her. She entered the conference room while Knowle waited until the gunfire and the screams began before walking away. The world dissolved into blackness again.

In the darkness, a voice rang in my head, one I knew belonged to the stoner with the full-face owl tattoo. "The time has come."

An instant later, I opened my eyes. It was still night, whether it was the same night or part of my dream-state, I wasn't sure. I had no sense of time, but after my disorientation vanished, I realized Al, Delinda and I were standing together in the now empty Cultural Affairs parking lot. I turned to ask Delinda if she was okay, but both she and Al were staring straight ahead, seemingly unaware of my presence. Meanwhile, the voice of the stoner continued to speak from inside my head. "All of you... Warriors from past and present, together with your ancient magic shall fight as one to avenge the Nukat." Another flash of blackness the world dissolved away once more.

When my vision finally cleared, I was still standing in the center of the asphalt lot. Now oddly enough, I was barefoot and naked except for the rough, leather loincloth fastened low around my hips. The skin of my legs and arms was dark, and my limbs were thick with ropy muscles. When I turned my head, I caught a glimpse of long, braided black hair resting atop my shoulders. It was then realized I was gripping something tightly in my hand. It was a stone knife. I discounted the fleeting thought I was still stoned and hallucinating. All of this felt very real.

A loud crack of thunder interrupted my epiphany. Then, the front doors of the Cultural Center flew open as if struck by a powerful wind from within. Knowle stumbled through the portal, still wearing the same suit and tie I saw when he gave the gun to Mercedes. Except now, he appeared to be in great pain, staggering slowly, and holding his head. In a weak voice, barely above a murmur, he moaned, "I can't control him... He's become too strong... He's..."

Mid-sentence, Knowle began gasping, his mouth wide open, gulping on the air like a landed fish. Crimson rivulets started streaming out of his eyes and nose. The blood came faster and faster, becoming thick streams that erupted into gushing geysers of red fluid. Howling in agony, he held his head even tighter, as if he were holding it together as his legs flew out from under him. But instead of falling to the pavement, he remained impossibly upright. His face was distorting, swelling outward until the skin could stretch no further. Finally, his entire countenance ripped open, bursting with a horrific sound of rending flesh so loud it drowned out his frantic, gurgling screams. Then, Knowle's entire body exploded into bloody fragments and what little meat was left behind sloughed off like a snake shedding its skin. Tahquitz, resurrected in his own physical presence now stood in the center of a puddle of gore that had once been a man.

Lean, heavily muscled and solidly built, the shaman was much taller than Knowle had been. His eyes were glowing like red coals inside his bald head, staring straight at me with animal-like intensity. I could tell our recognition was mutual, for his contorted expression radiated a savage hate that I realized had festered for centuries. In one hand he gripped the familiar, obsidian war ax and in the other a stone knife.

"Albok!" he roared, putting his head down as he charged towards me.

My enemy's abrupt move was not unexpected. I felt no confusion, nor fear. I was in control, and at the same time, I realized my reactions weren't purely my own. "Tacquish!" I bellowed, already running towards him, blade poised to strike the first blow.

Before we collided into each other, he swung his war ax. Instinctively, I ducked and narrowly avoided the brutal blow with reflexes I never knew I possessed. My focus wasn't on the ax head that whistled through the empty air only inches above where my head had been. Instead, I anticipated the inevitable next strike, twisting my body to avoid it, but I was too late. Tacquish had sensed my feint and had thrust upward with his knife, scribing a long, shallow cut from my belly button up to my sternum. Amazingly, I felt nothing, and when I looked down, I ·was again astonished. My wound had healed instantly.

Tacquish screamed with anger and surprise as my injury disappeared and struck again with the war ax. I turned to avoid it, but his weapon still neatly sliced into my left shoulder as I did. The shallow cut vanished instantaneously and then, with a skill set honed in countless battles I never fought in; I hurled myself into my foe, entangling his arms to prevent him from delivering yet another blow. We crashed onto the pavement, rolling and writhing as we struggled to break apart as to strike each other again with our weapons. I wrestled one arm free and smashed my fist into his face with all my might. Somehow, I knew there was Djinn's powerful magic in that blow in addition to my own physical strength.

Tacquish's head snapped back with the impact, striking the pavement hard enough to stun him momentarily. It was long enough for me to snatch the war ax away from his grasp. An instant later he recovered enough to roll free and regain his feet. I did the same, leaping to a standing position as he charged me again like a maddened bull.

Before he could traverse the short distance between us, I threw the ax with a skill that was never my own. The weapon struck him squarely in the forehead, burying itself deep into his skull. He should have fallen, mortally wounded, but he didn't. He grabbed the ironwood handle and began pulling it free from his head. I was suddenly cognizant of the stone blade in my hand, which had begun glowing a bright red as if it were on fire. Somewhere nearby, an owl began to sing loudly. As Tacquish finally managed to free the ax from his forehead, I flung myself into his midsection even as he raised it up to strike. With all my strength, I sunk my glowing blade hard into his stomach and jerked upwards.

Tacquish's horrific screams mixed with the screeching owl song, splitting the night air. The shaman, staring down at his hanging entrails, dropped the ax. The obsidian ax head shattered when it struck the ground. The stone knife I held was no longer glowing, but the edges of the long cut I had carved in the shaman's belly were radiating with a bright white light. Tacquish sunk to his knees, his eyes gleaming with hate. "Tennah ah meniken!"

"Senta moraka Muut acata," I spat back as I watched him fall forward onto the ground. The edges of his wound began to expand, and the white light became even more brilliant as it consumed Tacquish's entire body. Soon, all that remained was a bilious, vaporous mist. The owl continued to sing in victory as the world dissolved away.

CHAPTER NINETEEN

Palm Springs, California. Present Day.

WHEN I CAME TO, I wasn't sure where I was—or even who I was. After my eyes finally focused, I saw Al and Delinda kneeling beside me. "What the hell?" was the only response I could muster. My first realization was that I was lying on the ground, utterly disoriented. My second was that my head was pounding, and I felt like I was going to puke. It was still night although I had no idea of what time it was. I slowly sat up and looked around, noting that the three of us were alone in the desert. All of a sudden, memories flooded back into my brain like a bad movie. "Where's the dude in the Chevy?"

Delinda looked at me with a raised eyebrow. "What are you talking about?"

"You know what I'm talking about. Rosselli's thugs were going to kill us, right before the owl guy drove up in the Chevy and froze time." I looked at Al, whose expression reflected both confusion and concern. "Then he combined all of us together into an awesome Indian warrior to fight Tahquitz..." I looked over at Delinda and caught the worried look on her face. *Did they not remember?*

"Wow, that hit on the head really messed you up," said Al.

"It did? No, no... I remember!" Now the both of them were staring at me like I was from Mars. I was now more puzzled than ever. "Okay, Then, what really did happen?" I rubbed my head, and fresh blood came away on my hand.

Delinda examined my scalp before she and Al helped me get to my feet. "It doesn't look you'll need stitches," she pronounced. "But it's apparent that you have a concussion. A bad one, judging from your present state of mind."

"I'm all right, just a little sore… But, answer my question," I pressed in frustration. "How did we get here?"

Al and Delinda glanced at each other for a moment with mirrored expressions of disbelief. "You really don't remember?" Delinda said.

"Humor me," I replied.

"Well, after they knocked you out, the men drove us here and made us get out of the car… Then, after warning us to keep our mouths shut, they just left. All in all, considering that you upset some very dangerous people, we were very lucky."

"What?" I retorted. "They just left us?"

"Maybe they lost their nerve," Al offered. "But that's what happened." I waited for some indication they knew more than they were willing to admit, but they didn't even share a knowing glance.

At that moment I was nearly convinced I had merely imagined my entire experience until another memory bubbled up to the top of my consciousness. "Al, what does 'Senta moraka Muut acata' mean?"

Al looked at me like I had hit him with a hammer. "Where did you hear that?"

"Does it matter?"

Al cast a questioning look at Delinda before he answered. "It's in the old Ivia language…"

"So, what does it mean?" I asked, more frustrated than ever.

"Roughly, it means, 'Suffer Muut's eternal wraith.'"

"So, now do you believe that the owl guy made us into one person so we could fight Tacquish to the death?"

Delinda looked at me in a way I had never seen before. Was she upset? "Absolutely not," she insisted sharply.

"I have to admit, I'm not sure what to believe right now," said Al.

"So you believe me?"

"It's an interesting notion," Al replied.

"Ironic, isn't it? That only I remember?" I said.

Al laughed. "When you put it that way, it strikes me that the gods of the Iviatim have a sense of humor. What do you think Delinda?"

Delinda shook her head. "It's inconceivable that I wouldn't sense magic that powerful."

Did I imagine just a hint of willful denial in her reply? "Come on, Delinda... For the sake of argument, let's say it did happen the way I said it did. Perhaps there are powers out there greater than..."

"That is highly doubtful," Delinda interrupted tersely. She took a moment to stare up into the star-filled night sky as if it held the answer. Then she added, "But, not impossible."

Actually, I thought my recollection more plausible than the unlikely event that those two thugs had abandoned their plans to murder us in the desert. And of course, there was that phrase... With a start, I realized I couldn't bring it back into my head again. Al was right—the gods have a wicked sense of humor.

I refused to ponder all of this any longer as the part of my brain responsible for keeping me sane returned my attention to our present situation. "So, what do we do now?"

Delinda held up a mobile phone. I recognized it as mine. "You call for a ride."

"I don't think we can get an Uber in the middle of nowhere," I said as she handed it to me.

"We're not quite in the middle of nowhere... Take a look," she replied pointing to the nearby street sign. We were at the intersection of Sinatra and Royce. I glanced at my watch—it was only half past ten.

We had just gotten out of the Uber and entered the lobby of our hotel where we found Detective Hembling waiting for us. He eyed us suspiciously as he rose from the chair he was sitting in. "I know it's late, but I wanted to talk to you before you leave town." From the way he said it, there was little doubt it was more than just a suggestion.

"Oh," I replied. I wasn't surprised—we were not on his favorite people list.

147

"What the hell happened to you," Hembling asked, eyeing my blood-soaked hair.

"I got rolled by a couple of thugs," I said. I wasn't in the mood to be subtle.

Hembling raised his eyebrows in surprise. "They wouldn't happen to be a tall guy and a short guy would they?"

"Yeah, they would. How did you know?"

"We found them wandering around town, smashed to the gills. Both of 'em smelled like they inhaled an entire marijuana field. It might be legal, but being intoxicated in public isn't."

I must have looked completely taken aback, but Al jumped right in. "The short one hit Tonnick here hard in the head before they drove off."

"Drive? I'm impressed that they were able to manage that," chuckled Hembling. "They were so wasted they could hardly walk. Even without the added assault and battery charge, they won't be outside prison walls anytime soon... When we picked 'em up on a drunk and disorderly we discovered they were armed, in violation of their paroles. But that's not why I'm here."

I was about to mention Tommy Rosselli's role in all of this, but I figured he had already left town, confident his goons had eliminated us. While Hembling was talking, Delinda had wandered over to the bar and had returned with a bag of ice.

"What can we help you with, then?" Al asked.

"Thanks," I said as I took the bag she offered and applied it to what had become a very large bump.

"Ice pack for the second time in three days," she remarked. "It's almost becoming a habit."

Ignoring our sidebar, Hembling said, "I'll get right to the point then. What do you know about Miguel Knowle?"

I answered before anyone else did. "Not much, other than he was the one who contacted us on behalf of the Tribal Council. They wanted us to investigate a cable that they found on sacred land... One that wasn't supposed to be there. That's why we came out here. It was only after we discovered it was a fake that all hell started to break loose." When Hembling didn't respond, I asked, "So, did you find him?"

The detective didn't reply right away, a tactic that cops frequently use to see if you will volunteer more information, presumably to fill the silence. When it became apparent that we had nothing else to offer, he finally answered. "We did. And the evidence looks more and more like he's responsible for the kidnappings and probably a lot more."

"That explains why he initially didn't want to alert AC&C about the cable rumor," observed Delinda.

"That's right," I added. "Knowle said he was only contacting us at the insistence of the Tribal Council."

"When you were interacting with him, did he exhibit any strange or unusual behavior... Say anything?" Hembling asked.

"No, nothing," I lied. *Except wringing an owl's neck and summoning the dead.* "So, do you have any idea why he went to all the trouble to concoct such an elaborate ruse in the first place?"

"Good question," Hembling acknowledged. "But we won't be getting any answers from him."

"I thought you said you found him," said Al.

The portly detective shook his head. "Oh, we found him. At least parts of him."

"Huh?" I replied. I turned to observe the expressions on Delinda's and Al's faces. They didn't give anything away. I was convinced their neutral reactions were genuine.

"We think he suicided in front of the Cultural Center. Looked like he blew himself up with an explosive device of some sort. The tech guys are still working on it."

Good luck with that, I thought. I was still having trouble unseeing Knowle in his last moments, while at the same time, trying to appear as surprised as Al and Delinda were.

"That's awful! Did he leave a note?" Delinda asked.

"As a matter of fact, he did," Hembling replied. "He stuffed it into the crate with Kelsey Hall. A lot of what he wrote didn't make much sense, but he admitted to the abductions. He claimed he did it to get back at the families of those responsible for the Section 14 incident. Everyone who knew Knowle was aware his parents died in the fires back then, but none of them imagined he was capable of doing anything like this. I guess he held onto his anger for all these years until it was impossible for him to control it anymore. He blamed everyone that profited from Section 14, including people in his own tribe. Apparently, that was his motivation behind all of his crimes."

"Terrible," commented Delinda. "To punish the children for the sins of their parents."

"Sounds like a man possessed," I offered. Both Al and Delinda gave me that look. I have to say I enjoyed it.

"Oh, he was deranged all right. You should have seen the mess at his house. He was deep into some crazy Indian stuff. We're still trying to work out how he figured into Meena's and Schwartz's murder... And, how he talked Mercedes into shooting up the Tribal Council."

While parts of my "dream" had faded, there were still moments I could still vividly recall, but I refrained from mentioning them. I didn't think suggesting that Tahquitz's spirit could move from one person to another, like a supernatural Air-BnB, would get much traction. But it occurred to me for the first time that crazy theory might also shed some light on Meena's murder. I recalled that Schwartz had been the first one down the hill that day. If Knowle had followed us out to the dig, it might have provided an opportunity for Tahquitz's spirit to have taken hold of Schwartz as it had done with Mercedes.

That could explain why Schwartz appeared so disoriented when we first caught up with him. It was possible that he might have killed Meena under Tahquitz's influence and had no memory of it afterward. Maybe he retained some inkling of what he had done, but in any event, Knowle had likely killed him to seal his lips. I was surprised not only for coming up with these crazy explanations but thinking any of them might be even remotely true. Somewhere in my psyche a rabbit hole alert was sounding loud and clear.

There was one other detail... The mysterious sniper. "Detective, would you happen to know if Knowle had any military experience?"

"Humm. If I recall his file correctly, I think he was a Marine. Served in Iraq during the first invasion."

That was enough for me, another missing piece of the puzzle had just fallen into place. I remember in Marine Boot camp, they used to hand out marksman medals like candy at Halloween. At least that sounded rational. NOT TRUE !!!

"How are the girls?" Delinda asked. "Will they be okay?"

"We hope so," Hembling replied. "They're responding to treatment. It will be a few more days before we can question them completely." He stood up to leave. "All right. That's it. Have a safe trip home... I don't want to see you at any more crime scenes."

"Don't worry," I assured him. "Speaking for myself, I'm eager to get back to normal daytime temperatures." Although I still wanted more answers than Hembling could provide, I didn't need to be hanging around here to get them. More missing pieces of the puzzle were clicking together in my head.

After Hembling left, I turned to my friends. "Okay. I'm starting to think that I didn't imagine that owl god thing..."

"I think the blow to your head affected your memory," Delinda said. "Or, I wouldn't need to remind you that you don't believe in the supernatural..."

"For the sake of argument, let's say that somehow the owl god combined our skills and consciousnesses into one powerful Native American warrior to battle Tahquitz using magic and mad fighting skills."

"Are you listening to yourself?" Delinda asked. She was serious, if her wrinkled brow and concerned expression were any indications. "Maybe you do need to go to the hospital."

I held up my hand in hopes of dissuading that idea. "I'm fine! Really!"

"If you say so, Mark," Al said shaking his head. "But you gotta know, all of that sounds crazy, even to me."

If someone who claims to be thousands of years old is calling you nuts, then you probably are. "So, you two don't remember anything? Really?"

Nobody answered. To quote the construction guy who nearly drowned me in a shower of cement, *"Who am I to argue?"*

CHAPTER TWENTY

Baldwin Village, California. Present Day

I WAS GLAD DELINDA had offered to drive us back that same night. I wasn't sure why she was in a hurry to return to LA, but I had my suspicions. Perhaps the owl god experience had played a part in that. I could see how a sudden change in the supernatural pecking order, might prove unsettling to someone who considered herself high up the chain. Perhaps she was troubled because I could remember what she and Al couldn't. Whatever the reason, she had assured us she was ready to go as soon as Al and I were packed. That suited me fine—I had my fill of the desert.

Shortly after I had returned to my room to pack, I heard several soft knocks at my door. It was Delinda. "How are you feeling?" she asked.

"Like somebody hit me over the head with the butt of a gun," I replied, mildly surprised at her concern. Was her resolve weakening? I needed to know. "Delinda, I don't want you to take this the wrong way, but I want to ask you again. Where is our relationship going? Do we have one at all?"

I thought there was a flash of confusion in her eyes before she suddenly looked away. "We do... Just not in the way you imagine."

I turned and zipped up my overnight bag. "Okay, I think I get it. Really, I do... But, I need to know why." Then it struck me. "Is there anyone else?"

Before she closed the door behind her, she answered in a voice barely above a whisper. "No. No one else."

I really hadn't thought about what I expected, but I was beginning to realize how complicated our relationship had become. Despite that, I resolved not to let the issue drive a wedge between us. Any future with Delinda was better than none—a thought that surprised me. I would have never figured myself as one who harbored any romantic tendencies. After one failed marriage and a bunch of relationships that had gone nowhere fast, I wasn't even sure what I was hoping for. All I could do was wait and see.

On the long drive back to LA, Al and I began discussing several more details about the Section 14 case. In the interests of sanity, namely my own, my brain had kicked my supernatural theories to the curb in favor of more rational reasonings. Not that I really thought these explanations were better, but at least they had nothing to do with evil ghosts, gods or spirit possession. The conversation also kept my mind off of Delinda's insane driving.

"You wonder how somebody like Knowle would snap like that," Al said, shaking his head.

"Hell, that kind of crazy doesn't just happen overnight," I replied. "Knowle planned his revenge for a very long time. He needed a cover for his kidnapping, so he used the Tahquitz legend to issue to panic the tribal community and direct everyone's attention elsewhere. The cooked up the cable story was to explain how Tahquitz had risen from the dead."

"Well, it worked," said Al. "And evidently he killed Meena to keep her from revealing who put her up to planting the fake cable?"

"Yeah, and I'll bet she also had a hand in spreading the story," I ventured. "She was a student, and probably needed money, so I'm sure Knowle made it worth her while. But he knew she'd come clean with the truth once we found out the cable was bullshit. He couldn't afford to be connected in any way. At least, not until his revenge was complete."

"Then, what was the point of shooting at us?" Al cracked a thin smile. "I mean, at you?"

"More intimidation," I ventured. "Maybe my superior skills of deduction worried him." I ignored Al's dismissive snort. "Or, maybe he was trying to scare us off. Once he realized that wasn't going to work, he killed Schwartz to make it harder for us to discount the cable and its connection to Tahquitz... No one in the tribal community was going to take our word for it."

"But what about the girls?" Delinda asked. "Why did he bother to keep them alive?"

"Probably for the shock value," I replied. "Most likely, Knowle kept them locked up somewhere in the Cultural Center. He wanted them alive, so they'd be relatively 'fresh' when those crates arrived at the Smithsonian."

"He must have realized that he'd be found out in any event," Delinda said.

"Yeah," I replied. "Eventually, it was all going to lead back to him."

"So, he planned to kill himself all along." Delinda shook her head in disgust. "What a sick, sick man."

"You've got it figured, Mark," Al said slyly. "Very logical... All things considered."

"Yes, all things considered," I agreed, ignoring his sarcasm.

"Except you left out a few things, like Tacquish and your encounter with the owl god."

I shrugged off his observation. "I'm not going there. In any event, we've wrapped this up. AC&C is in the clear, and the bad guy is dead."

"That leaves your other case" Delinda took her eyes off the road for one terrifying moment to spare me a withering look. "The one that nearly got you killed."

"Well, I'm sorry I got you both involved in that. As soon as you drop me off, I'm going to get right on it."

"Not by yourself, you're not," Al said with a shake of his head. "I think you're gonna need our help." I started to argue, but I never got the chance.

"Absolutely," interjected Delinda.

"I'm not splitting my fee," I countered.

"Ha, ha," Al cracked. "You can buy us dinner on somebody else's expense account."

I ignored him, but truth be told, I welcomed their willingness to lend a hand. My impossibly wild dream, courtesy of the stoner in the Chevy had shown me that certain occasions, three heads were better than one. I remained silent for a few seconds to give the impression I had been dragged kicking and screaming to agree. I could tell from Al's expression I wasn't fooling anybody.

"All right then, if you both insist on helping me, I think we should begin by having a chat with the evidence clerk, Evan Gonzales."

Al jumped right in. "Sounds like a plan!"

Delinda pulled her phone from her purse. "I can get his address."

"Hold on!" I tried to keep the panic out of my voice, but she was already punching buttons on her mobile with one hand while she flew effortlessly around slower traffic.

"Got it," she said triumphantly. "We'll head straight over. Should be there around breakfast time. Probably a good time to catch him at home."

"I think all of this has turned you guys into a bunch of action junkies!"

Al laughed at my jibe. "Maybe."

Evan Gonzales's address was in a quiet, suburban neighborhood located in the southernmost portion of Baldwin Hills, just outside the Los Angeles City Limits. Known as Baldwin Village since the late '90s, it's a diverse, blue-collar residential area dotted with apartments and condos. While most of the architecture is nondescript, the prevailing landscape of tropical plantings and other "jungle-esque" flora give the community a certain amount of character.

It was shortly after eight in the morning that we drove up to Gonzales's duplex—arriving just in time to see the coroner's wagon pull away from the front of the residence.

I tried to keep the disappointment out of my voice. "Why do I think Tommy's thugs tied up this loose end before they went on vacation in the Springs?" Too bad, I thought. Gonzales was probably Brent Todd's best—and only hope of proving his innocence.

Now, only a single patrol car remained on scene. I rolled down my window as we came up alongside the cruiser and greeted the two cops inside with a tone I hoped would convey both concern and sincerity. "Hello, Officers. I live down the street. Is everything all right?"

The cop looked up from the clipboard he was scribbling on before he replied. "Everything is under control."

"May I ask what happened?"

The officer clearly wasn't happy to be interrupted while filling out his paperwork. "There was an accident here last night... Gas leak." He motioned with his head to the Gas Company truck parked across the street. "They've got it fixed. There's no danger of an explosion."

"That's good news," I said, sounding suitably relieved. "Was anyone hurt?"

The cop hesitated as though he was weighing the wisdom of giving me an answer versus ordering me to go away. Relenting, he said, "I'm afraid so. There was a woman in the house. That's all I can tell you."

I gave him a solemn nod. "So sorry to hear that," I offered before we drove on.

"Does that mean our loose end is alive?" Al mused. "Where do you think we can find him?"

A car passed us quickly going in the opposite direction and pulled up into the driveway of the Gonzales house. "I believe we just did," I replied. "Delinda, if you can find a place to park, we should wait for an opportunity to talk to him."

Just like magic, she found a curbside spot that offered a clear view of the duplex. We watched from down the street as Gonzales, still in uniform, got out of his car and ran over to his front door, only to be intercepted by the cops I had just spoken with. Understandably, he became visibly upset as they told them what had happened. Since, for whatever reason, he wasn't home when the "accident" occurred, he avoided the fate of the woman who had been carried off the coroner's van. Having said that, it was easy to make an educated guess as to who was taking the trip to the morgue.

Twenty minutes later, both the patrol car and the gas company truck had driven away, leaving Gonzales alone to deal with his grief and the aftermath of the tragedy. He was sitting on the front steps of his house, holding his hands in his head when the three of us walked up to him.

He was short and stocky, well past the verge of being overweight. The buttons on his ill-fitting uniform were stretching back and forth with each of his pitiful sobs. From his name I expected him to be Latino, but apparently, his heritage was primarily African American.

"Evan Gonzales? Sorry for your loss," I began. "But, you realize this wasn't an accident."

"Who are you," he retorted, looking up at us with reddened eyes as tears streamed down his cheeks. His grief was palpable and heartfelt, and at that moment I honestly felt sorry for the guy. I've seen this all too many times—one lousy decision having led to another until there was no turning back. Resulting in lives that were changed forever, and never for the better.

"I'm Mark Tonnick, and these are my associates, Delinda, and Al. Believe me, I know this can't be a good time, but we need to talk."

"I already know it wasn't an accident… The gas guys think my wife committed suicide…" He fought back another involuntary sob. "I know things have been tough, with her cancer and our finances… But I never expected this."

I only had one card to play—and it involved jumping to a conclusion that was only partially based on hard facts. But, I played it anyway. "You don't understand," I said softly. "Tommy Rosselli did this to keep you from talking. He expected you would be at home. Your wife was collateral damage."

Gonzales looked up at us. The expression on his face was a mixture of fear and confusion. "What?"

"We know about the payoff," Al said. "You were a loose end that could have tied everything back to him."

"Holy shit!" Gonzales squeezed his eyes shut as if he could make everything go away. When he opened them again, they were full of rage. "That Asshole! I wouldn't have said anything!"

"There was too much was at stake to take you at your word," I said. "Dead men tell no tales."

"~~Motherfucker~~! I was working a double shift, or I would have been here!"

"If you want to stay alive," Delinda said. "You need to tell the truth about Rosselli's scheme to frame…" She glanced my way.

"Detective Brent Todd," I prompted. "You're going to be called to testify at his IA hearing. If you come clean, Rosselli will go down for this… And more."

"Yeah? Well, so will I," Gonzales protested. "I'll lose my job and my pension."

"Maybe," I countered. "But you won't send an innocent man to prison and let your wife's murder go unavenged."

"Think about it," said Delinda gently.

"Also, I'd keep a low profile until then. If Rosselli finds out you're still alive, he'll try again… He's that kind of guy."

Gonzales nodded. "I'll think about it."

I figured it was time to go. If push came to shove, we could sweat the truth out of him at the hearing since we knew the whole story. Like most of my cases, what started out as simple ended up as a full-on shit-storm. As we walked back to the Benz, I reflected on Gonzales and reminded myself I was no one to judge. Some people are more imperfect than others, but it doesn't mean they always deserve what happens to them. I'll admit that trying not to give a damn has always been the hardest part of my job.

None of us spoke for a long while after we got into the car and drove away. Despite my reluctance, I found myself wishing for a magical solution to make everyone whole again. I suppose you can't walk in pixie dust without getting it on your shoes.

CHAPTER TWENTY-ONE

Los Angeles, California.   Present Day

DELINDA AND AL DROPPED me off in front of my office around noon.   Willie saw me come in and flagged me down right after I stopped to open my mailbox.

"Hey, Tonnick, you owe me thirty bucks."

"Huh?" I replied, sorting through the sheaf of mail, looking for checks. As usual, I was disappointed. "What for?"

"Cat food, a cat box, and a few other accessories."   Willy was grinning.   "You gotta take care of your pet.   You don't want her peeing in the hallway!"

"She's not my pet!" I protested.   "She just walked in and made herself at home.   I was hoping she'd be gone by the time I got back."

"Come on, Mark.   A little responsibility will do you good."

I shook my head and waved him off as I headed up the stairs to my office.   "Thanks for nothing, Willie.   Maybe I'll send her down so you can take care of her!"

My office door was unlocked, which was no big surprise.   I had left it slightly ajar in the hopes the freeloading feline would take off for better digs.   Those aspirations were dashed the moment I walked in. The cat who had been asleep in my chair, awoke and wisely jumped under the couch at my approach.   Willie had indeed seen to her creature comforts.   Lined up against the wall opposite the couch were a plastic cat litter-box and a set of matching ceramic kibble and water bowls decorated with pink, kitty paw prints.

"Well, I guess I'm stuck with you," I said, addressing the cat who was eyeing me warily from where she had taken refuge.   She gave me a questioning "m'wrarr," a response I hadn't been expecting. "So, you'll probably be expecting a name, right?"

I got another, similar reply as the cat ventured slowly out from under the couch towards where I had taken a seat at my desk. "Okay, what shall it be then?"

Then, without warning, the damn thing jumped up into my lap and started purring. "Hey, I don't remember inviting you to the party," I said. But it was too late. She laid down in my lap and started nuzzling her head into my hands. "Okay, let's keep this professional." I knew at that moment, she was as Willie said, my cat.

"Okay… So what should I call you?" I knew she wasn't going to present me with any suggestions, so I said the first name that came into my mind. "How about, 'Ruby?'" She stopped purring long enough to give me another "m'wrarr," which was good enough for me. Ruby, it was. My mobile rang, and at the sound, Ruby jumped off of my lap and moved over to the couch. On top of it this time, not under it. By mutual agreement we had reached detente.

It was Todd. "What have you got for me, Tonnick? My hearing has been moved up to tomorrow."

"I think you better sit down, Brent. What I've got to tell you isn't pretty." It took me barely ten minutes to lay out the entire sordid mess for him. Lisa and Rosselli, the faked video, the crooked evidence clerk, the connection to his dead uncle and all the rest.

"Un-fucking-believable!" he said once I was finished. "And Lisa was in on it!?"

"Yeah, I'm afraid so."

"Shit!" There was silence as he processed everything I had told him. Finally, he asked, "So, how do we prove it?"

"I think the evidence clerk will come clean. Rosselli tried to off him, but killed the guy's wife instead."

"Christ almighty! But, what if the guy is too scared to tell the truth?"

"Then, I also have two witnesses, besides myself, that heard Rosselli confess to practically everything. Bring your uncle's will, that will prove motive and help to corroborate the rest of it."

"Will do." There was another brief silence, followed by, "Tonnick, I won't forget this."

I hoped he meant that in a positive way. "First, let's get you off the hook. What time did they schedule the hearing for?"

"Ten, at the Van Nuys Courthouse. My union rep and my attorney will be there too."

"I'll bring my two associates. I guarantee they'll be quite convincing."

I called Delinda and told her about Brent Todd's hearing in the morning. She promised to bring Al and meet me there a half-hour before the proceedings were scheduled. I was hoping that Todd's case would be resolved quickly once we all testified. If Rosselli was half as smart as I thought he was, he'd already be taking the shortest route he could find out of town.

I sat at my desk going through my end of the month bills feeling pretty good. One case was resolved, and another would be put to rest soon enough. Even better, over the last few months, I was able to catch up with all of my past-due bills. Thanks to Ashton and his AC&C business, I had money in my checking account for the first time in my career—a whole new experience.

As I was reflecting on my recent good fortune, Ruby started to hiss loudly for no apparent reason at the exact same time the scar on my cheek began burning. I had no reason for what I did next, but those events galvanized me into action.

Immediately, I dropped to the floor and shimmied underneath the couch next to where Ruby was hiding. In the next instant, a dozen shots tore through my office door, squarely striking the back of the chair I had just quit. Then, mere seconds later, the shooting stopped as abruptly as it had begun.

After waiting for several more moments, I crawled out from the cover of the couch as silently as I could manage and positioned myself behind the door jamb. Whoever was gunning for me would surely have sense enough to make sure they finished the job properly—basic "Hitman 101."

Unfortunately, I was right. The assailant's kick blew open the splintered door with a louder bang than the suppressed rounds he had just fired. Confronted by the sight of my empty office, the guy cautiously entered for a better look. For no reason at all, Ruby jumped up onto the desk with an ear-splitting screech, distracting the shooter long enough for me to make my move. I slammed into him shoulder first, at the same time I grabbed his gun arm and wrestled it downward.

I was lucky. The guy was thin and wiry—I outweighed him by about thirty pounds or more. My grip on his arm, in tandem with my weight and momentum, took him down to the floor fast. On the way, his head struck the brass doorknob on the open door, stunning him—but not enough to make him let go of the gun. I grabbed the closest thing I could find, an old lamp on the end table next to the couch, and smashed him full in the face with it. Unfortunately for him, the shade didn't do much to protect the CFL bulb. It shattered along with several of his teeth, and I'm sure the toxic gas he got a good whiff of wasn't therapeutic in any way, either. My would-be assassin crumpled onto the floor, bloody and senseless.

About the same time, Willie ran up the stairs with one of the double-barreled shotguns he keeps locked up in a display case behind the counter. "Shit! I was just locking up when I heard the commotion and grabbed up some iron." He looked at the guy on the floor. "Not an admirer, I take it."

"Not so much," I replied.

Willy took another moment and surveyed my ruined office. There were bullet holes everywhere. "Jesus Tonnick, how did you not get hit?"

"Believe it or not, the cat saved my life."

"Well, I'll be damned!" Willy swore. "You are one lucky somoabitch!"

"That I am," I agreed. I grabbed a handful of zip ties from a desk drawer and used them to bind the hands of my unconscious intruder.

There was no need to call 911 since a bevy of cops arrived about five minutes later.   They said an anonymous good samaritan had recognized the silenced rounds for what they were and called in a shots fired report.

I happily explained the entire chain of events, and since they wisely determined it was unlikely I would shoot up my own office, they left the zip ties in place while they waited for the ambulance. The guy wasn't going anywhere anyway—he was still out cold, and it looked like his unplanned rendezvous with my lamp had broken his jaw. That was too bad since he wouldn't be able to talk about who put him up to the job anytime soon. Not that I needed to ask.

It was abundantly clear to me that Tommy the Shark was looking to tie up more loose ends. That's when the realization hit me. I punched in Todd's number and let it ring five or six times before it went to voicemail. If Rosselli was worried that his plans to frame Brent Todd were rapidly falling apart, he might be tempted to fall back on a more direct approach.

I told the cop who had been taking my statement that one of their own might be in danger and quickly explained why. Whether he knew anything about Brent Todd's situation or if he was merely reacting to the urgency in my voice, he took what I was telling him seriously. I hadn't even finished before he called it in on his chest mic. I heard the confirming reply on his belt radio. Local patrol was on their way over to Todd's midtown condo. I just hoped they weren't too late.

I didn't bother waiting for the last of the cops to leave before I hustled down the stairs and out the back door of the building where I park my Toyota. Usually, the locals leave my junker alone, but today of all days, every one of the four tires was gone along with the front seats and the steering wheel. The remains were left suspended on cinderblocks apparently pilfered from the nearby wall. I was willing to bet if I had the time to take a closer look I'd also find that critical engine parts were missing. I pulled out my mobile and got Delinda on the line.

"Hey, where are you?" I didn't bother with a greeting.

"Why?"

"My car is hosed, and I need to get over to Brent Todd's place right away. I think he may be in trouble. Cops are already headed over there."

Her reaction was as direct as my request. "Take an Uber... Al and I will meet you." She rang off before I could even give her the address.

Less than four minutes later I piled into the Uber driver's Sentra, and we made for Todd's address. Uncharacteristically, traffic was light, and we arrived at Todd's midtown condo in just under twenty minutes. As I hurried out of the car, I saw Delinda's Mercedes was parked nearby.

"Good thing you alerted the police. They got to him just in time," Delinda's voice said from behind me.

I turned to see her and Al. "Was he shot?" I asked.

Al shook his head, "No, he was on the verge of dying from an overdose."

"Whoever did it was trying to make it look like he did it on purpose," Delinda added.

"Did they give him Narcan?" I ventured. Police on patrol in LA routinely carry the opioid antidote since they need it all too often.

She shrugged. "They must have since he's still alive. They were taking him to the ER when we got here. We were waiting for you, thinking you'd probably want to go over to the hospital."

"Yeah, that's a plan," I agreed as we made for her car.

Kaiser Hospital is on Sunset Boulevard, a little more than a mile from where we were. Like most big-city emergency rooms, Kaiser's backlog of patients waiting for medical attention depended on many variables that change by the minute. Accidents, walk-ins, and crime victims all vie for a slot in a perennially overloaded medical system.

Not surprisingly, getting folks out the door is equally, if not more important than getting them in.

I lied to the security guard at the front desk and said I was Brent Todd's brother-in-law, adding that Al and Delinda were also related. I'm not sure he believed me, but he didn't care enough to press the issue.

We entered the emergency waiting room area just as Todd was being released. That wasn't surprising as recovery from an overdose with Narcan is nearly instantaneous.

He spotted us immediately. "Tonnick?"

"What the hell happened?" I asked.

"I came home from dinner out, and two guys were waiting for me inside. They jumped me right after I walked in the door. The next thing I know, I'm being loaded into an ambulance."

"I had the police check on you after some guy shot up my office," I said. "I figured you were on Rosselli's list."

"Good thing you did. They said they found me with the needle still in my arm."

"Maybe Rosselli thought he could make it look like a suicide," I ventured.

Todd nodded. "Yeah, like I was so despondent about my IA hearing... Except for one thing... It's been canceled. I was going to call you, except all this went down first."

"What happened?"

"Gonzales, the evidence clerk gave it all up. After his wife was killed, he turned himself in and asked for protective custody. He ended up confessing everything. I'm in the clear."

"Nice," I said. "I guess you can retire a rich man."

"Hardly. The Feds have already seized my uncle's money, seeing it's all illegal. I won't be rolling in the dough for the foreseeable future."

Shit... There goes my payday.

CHAPTER TWENTY-TWO

Epilogue

THE NEXT MORNING, I arrived at my office building in time to meet my landlord, who I had called the night before. Needless to say, he was extremely distressed about the condition of my office and even threatened me with eviction. He became more reasonable when I reminded him that he wrote the terms of my lease, which were reasonably iron-clad. Since technically, what had happened would be considered vandalism, I also advised him it was likely covered by his insurance. However, what really settled him down was my offer to cover his deductible.

Since the other two offices on the 2nd floor next to mine had stood vacant for the last several months, I knew my cheapskate landlord wasn't really all that eager to get rid of me. He also made a point of ignoring the kitty litter box before he left, muttering to himself about "no pets" as he retreated down the stairs. If that had ever come up, I was ready to point out the building's rat problem.

Earlier that morning, I had bought some heavy cream from Mrs. Krenzman, some of which I now poured into Ruby's bowl. She certainly had earned it. Willie had offered me one of the office chairs from his pawned stash of furniture since mine was in splinters. I sat down in it at my desk and surveyed my ruined office as my watch-cat started in on her reward. It was time to remodel the place in any event, and I was confident I'd be able to afford it, thanks to AC&C's continued patronage.

I returned to finishing up the bills from the night before and was licking the flap on the last envelope when my mobile rang. It was Brent Todd.

"Hey, they just picked up Rosselli at the Camarillo Airport. Somebody must have tipped him off that his inside man had flipped. He had booked a private jet and was on his way out of the country."

"No big surprise there," I said. "Glad to hear he didn't get away." Although I knew it would likely be a touchy subject, I still had to ask. "What about Lisa?"

Todd chuckled. "Once Rosselli figured the jig was up, he left her high and dry... She was waiting for him to show up at LAX when they found her."

I remembered what Rosselli said he had in mind for her. "Lucky girl... She could have ended up dead."

"No so lucky... They arrested her for accessory after the fact, and a whole list of other charges."

"Sorry to hear that," I offered.

"Hey, I'm not. If you hadn't figured it all out, I'd be the one going to jail, and she'd be gallivanting off with Rosselli. I've already hired a lawyer to file for divorce."

"Glad to hear everything worked out for the best, then. I'll send you my bill."

"Hey... Go easy! Remember, I've got to make do on a cop's salary."

"Just be glad I'm not including my office rehab," I said before ringing off.

I looked up and saw Delinda standing in my doorway, appraising the condition of my surroundings.

"Hey, what do you think? I call it 'nouveau target range,' the very latest in interior design."

"Somehow, I think it fits you," she replied just as Ruby jumped up into my lap. There was that smirk again. "I see you've made peace with your cat."

"It's a long story," I replied. "I can tell you over dinner tonight."

Delinda sighed. "You're incorrigible, Mark."

"I know. Almost getting killed brings out the best in me."

She brushed some plaster off of the couch and sat down. "You have to stop. I know how you feel about me, I really do, but..."

I didn't let her finish. "Well then, what's the problem?" Ruby jumped off of my lap as I quit my chair and took a seat beside Delinda on the couch.

"I'm not as real as you think," she said quietly.

"What are you talking about? You're as real as I am." I leaned in to kiss her, but my lips met nothing but air. When I opened my eyes, I was sitting alone on the couch. My mobile starting ringing on the desk. I let it ring several times before I got up to answer it.

It was Delinda. "Never try that again," she began. Maybe it was projection on my part, but I thought she sounded as disappointed as I was. "Please. For both our sakes."

I stood there, numbed—more from her rebuke than from her vanishing act, but somehow I summoned up the courage to tell her once more how I felt. "Delinda, there's not enough magic in the world to stop me from loving you." I waited for a reply, but she had already rung off. I looked over at the cat who staring up at me. "Guess it's just you and me for now, Ruby."

She replied with a soft meow. A second later my phone rang again. I was hoping it was Delinda, but it wasn't. It was Al.

"Hey Mark, I have some good news for you."

"I could use some. What's up."

Al chuckled. "Well, for starters, Ashton is sending over a company car for you to use. Also, he's including a bonus in your check this month."

"Wow, that is good news," I replied, genuinely impressed. "I guess we did good."

"You did good," Al said. "If it weren't for you, those girls would have died, and AC&C would have taken a public relations hit. Besides all that, I have to admit, I really enjoyed the excitement. I'm looking forward to the opportunity to work with you again."

"Thanks, Al, but I'm hoping things calm down around here for a while. I could use a lot less adrenaline in my daily diet." I paused to have a short debate inside my brain about whether to bring up something more personal. "Say, can I ask you for some advice... About Delinda?"

He sighed loudly into the phone. "Not much I can help you with there. I know you don't want to hear it, but she can't be with you... At least in the way you'd want it."

"That's what she says... But..."

"No buts, Mark. It's impossible. You'll have to leave it at that."

"Because she's a genie, right?"

"An ifrit," Al corrected.

Damn, I had been hoping this conversation wouldn't end up with another trip down the rabbit hole.

"Sorry. I know how much she means to you, but you'll just have to be happy with the way things are. From what I know, it would be dangerous."

"Dangerous? What are you talking about?"

"Mark, it's complicated, and frankly, you wouldn't believe it, so there's no point in going on about it." His voice softened when he added, "Don't put the blame on Delinda, I think she's as miserable about it as you are."

That didn't make me feel any better, but I saw no reason to press him further—that was all I was going to get. "Thanks, Al. I appreciate you telling me that. And don't forget to let Ashton know that I'm very grateful for his generosity."

"I'll tell him." Al paused before he added, "You take care, Mark," and clicked off.

I allowed myself to indulge in a long exhale of resignation and surveyed the mess around me. My eyes settled on the cat. While I had been on the phone, she had jumped onto the couch next to me and was now comfortably curled up asleep. An island of serenity surrounded by the ruins of my office.

I rose without disturbing Ruby's slumber and quietly headed down the stairs. Willy had promised to hook me up with a good contractor, and I was eager to put my place back in order. As ample testimony to either my stubbornness or my stupidity, I was already thinking about enlisting Delinda to help me with the redecorating.

I also intended to visit an old bookstore downtown that specialized in all things occult to see what I could learn about the care and feeding of "ifrits." After all the events over the last few days, what's another rabbit hole? Especially among friends.

A Note From the Author

The real history and legends of the Cahuilla Nation are an integral part of California's past. I have fictionalized many aspects of those in creating this novel with no intention of disrespect or cultural appropriation. However, some of the injustices suffered by the tribes and described in the story are based on historical events. I would encourage everyone to delve into the Cahuilla's real history for a richer understanding of their culture and heritage.

About the Author

Steve Zuckerman has had a long career as a music composer, orchestrator, and author. He began his musical career at nineteen, writing and creating the soundtracks for many "Sesame Street" animated shorts. He has also scored films ranging from the uber-campy "Spawn of the Slithis" to the super-sweet "Winnie the Pooh and a Day for Eeyore." Additionally, he's created hundreds of television commercials and has published numerous short stories and novels. He and his wife make their home in California, and spend much of their time traveling and visiting family in Arizona and Alaska.